# DARK FEATHERS

## NATALINA REIS

# DARK FEATHERS

# PROLOGUE

## NIX

I am darkness.

Darkness is all I know—it's what I do, what I breathe, what sustains me.

I've no memory of a time before the darkness, and I refuse to wonder about it. Death and pain surround me from dusk until dawn. The screams of horror, cries of despair, yet nothing touches me. I am numb.

I obey my master and stay alive. I don't remember why I want to live. I feel nothing and don't look forward to anything.

I merely exist—a hollow shell of whatever I was before. A lost soul, they call me. I don't know who they are or why I remember the words and not the faces, but I don't care.

I wake up from someone's nightmare into my own. There is

no light, no hope; all is dark. I am what my master made me—a creature of evil, a carrier of pain.

In darkness I dwell, and darkness I am.

# CHAPTER 1

## PLUCKING

## NIX

The shadows were longer now, but I was in no hurry. I had no reason to rush, nowhere to go. Crouched behind the trees, I waited. Like a crow hovering over a dying creature, I lingered, still and silent. The street was busy as the suburban dwellers rushed home to their families. Cars zoomed by, blurred and noisy, the reek of exhaust surrounding me in a toxic cloud. It didn't bother me. I would wait patiently until my target was ready for the plucking.

"Why are you hiding there?" The voice startled me. Was she talking to me? Not possible. And yet…. "Well, what the fuck are you doing there?"

The girl stared in my direction as if she could see me, her dark inquiring eyes trained on mine. I glanced around me, searching for someone else she may be talking to, but there was no one near. Annoyed, I looked away from her, dismissing the fancy notion that she could actually see me.

"You're creeping me out, dude. I'm going to call the police." She took a phone from her coat pocket and began punching numbers.

Crazy. Only crazy people talked to themselves.

But I couldn't deny that nagging feeling that she could indeed see me. Could angels go crazy?

My target appeared around the corner, his tall and thin body propelled by the urgency of the chase, head turned back to where two policemen pursued him on foot. Blinded by fear, he jumped over the curb and directly in front of a speeding white van. The screeching of tires caught the attention of the crazy girl, who dropped her hands along her sides and yelled in horror as the vehicle crashed against the body of the runner. The momentum of the impact threw him a few feet up in the air only to drop him seconds later in a heap of twisted arms and legs, blood pooling quickly around him.

The girl ran toward the dead man, phone forgotten in her hand, a litany of oh-my-gods in a trail behind her.

Crazy woman.

I straightened up and prepared to do what I was there for. In one long sweeping motion, I unfurled my black wings and flew the short distance to the prostrated figure on the road. The man's soul was peeking already, hesitant and blurry as they normally were, still stunned by sudden death. I wasted no time and reached out to grab him, my hands under his armpits. One sharp pull and his soul was freed from his lifeless body.

"What do you think you're doing? He still has a pulse." The crazy girl, now kneeling beside the body, looked at me. "Don't take him yet."

I almost dropped his soul. "You can see me?" My voice came out rough from lack of use. I couldn't remember the last time I had spoken. Dark angels didn't speak to each other, and our masters were not great talkers either.

She stood and looked up at me, not a bit scared or surprised. "Of course I can see you. Let the man go."

Confused and not used to being addressed, I stalled for a moment. "He's dead."

"Why are you taking him to the dark? What has he done?"

I didn't have to answer because the two police officers chasing him arrived at the scene. The dark-haired girl looked away long enough for me to escape, soul in tow, up into the heavens.

As I rose upward, I couldn't help but watch the mortal girl talk to the newly arrived men. How could she see me? No mortal had ever seen me before. Was that even possible?

Before I vanished behind the first layer of clouds, I saw her lift her eyes in my direction, and something inside of me cracked. For the first time ever, I wished to be remembered, to be seen.

Where was that coming from? And why was my cold heart quivering, longing for warmth? My world was not one for sentiment. Feelings were something I heard about but never experienced—at least not that I could remember. But then again, I didn't remember much. My days were a succession of tasks—mostly pluckings like this one—followed by a dreamless slumber. This reaction was unsettling, and the simple fact that I found it to be so was in itself upsetting.

The girl's eyes had followed me all the way to the clouds—not girl, woman. She was definitely a grown woman despite her size. I wasn't able to shake her from my thoughts. She was with me when I crossed the tar-black walls and still there as I dragged the now-whimpering soul through the large, dark foyer and into the holding cells. Normally I wouldn't even hear the insistent pleading of the plucked soul, but this time it was burning a hole inside me, an unpleasant tightening in my gut.

"Shut up," I yelled, unable to stand the distressing gnawing at my heart anymore. Several heads turned in my direction, surprised as much as I was by the sound of my voice. Dark angels normally existed with their eyes on the ground and their voices silent. I caught myself and tucked my chin to my chest, pretending it wasn't me. But the tugging at my heart only grew stronger as the soul of the criminal I had reaped continued to beg for mercy. I whispered to him, "Mercy is not mine to give. You chose this path a long time ago. Now you must pay your dues."

I had never spoken to a plucked soul. Ever! What had come over me? What had that short, crazy woman done to me?

After securing the soul in the forever containers, I needed to relate what had happened to my master. It was my duty to let him know of any unusual occurrences, but I found myself stalling for time, slowing my pace, finding excuses to delay my arrival at his office. His workspace was not what humans would call an office. Like most rooms inside the Dark Fortress, his was dark with walls made of a viscous black substance that reflected what went on between them. From the ceiling hung chains and shackles that matched those attached to the floor where Asmodeus tortured souls, often entertaining himself and his closest servants. Not that I felt sorry for the tortured souls, but unlike most of the other angels, I didn't have an appetite for cruelty. The room was a familiar space nevertheless, one where I myself was often toyed with, one I'd rather not enter or think about.

Asmodeus didn't bother looking up as I walked in, my wings still unfurled and dragging on the ground behind me. "The world better be coming to an end," he growled, his eyes never leaving the silver dagger he was meticulously honing on a big rock, "or you will regret having interrupted me."

I fell to one knee, my head nearly hitting the floor as I bowed down in submission. A shiver went through me as I contemplated what he might do to me if he so pleased. I was not afraid of death— it was virtually impossible to kill an angel—but Asmodeus was famous for much more horrifying options. I had tasted his wrath more than once and had no wish to do it again.

"Master, something odd happened during my last plucking." Much to my dismay, the words spilled out of my mouth in a weak and wavering stream. "A nearby mortal saw me."

His large red eyes rose and trained on me, the instant fingers of fear tightening around my neck. "What is this you tell me? Did you forget to charm yourself on the way down?"

Under the weight of his glare, I plunged even closer to the ground. "No, Master. My charms were up and working. She was the only one who could see me. And...." My voice trailed off as I realized one other strange detail.

My master growled louder, a sound that made my insides vibrate and contract in terror. "And what?" He stood up and strode toward me. "Stupid fucking minion, and what?"

"She didn't seem surprised I was collecting a soul." The words erupted from my mouth in a rush of syllables, all fighting for supremacy. I chanced a glance at Asmodeus, standing tall, dark, and threatening. For a moment I was frozen by the terrible beauty that was my master, his opalescent skin in stark contrast with his jet-black wings he unfurled as he walked to me.

Was that surprise on his face?

If it was, he disguised it quickly. He stopped and cupped his chin. "No surprise? Maybe she thought you were in costume."

I lowered my head again. "She asked me not to take his soul. She knew who I was and what I was doing there." This was not the conversation I wanted to have with the monster in charge of the Dark Fortress, but I had no choice. Better to tell him now than suffer the consequences of hiding the information.

"Who was she?" His voice was barely audible, and that scared me more than anything else.

"I don't know, Master. She appeared suddenly out of nowhere."

I didn't dare look up and meet his angry gaze, but there was no raging, no noise at all. Asmodeus was thinking.

"Angel, you are to find her, follow her, and find out why she can see you." That was not what I was expecting at all. "You will disguise yourself as a mortal and be her shadow until you find out. We can't have mortals walking around seeing our angels."

A knot formed in my throat, and I found it difficult to speak. "Yes, Master."

"Report to the Department of Intelligence for further directions." He was quiet and I didn't move, not sure if I was being dismissed. "What the fuck are you waiting for? Go!"

I rushed out of his office, confused and worried. What had I gotten myself into?

✝

## JOAN

"You guys are so cheesy." My big brother and his boyfriend were the cutest couple ever, but I was not about to tell them that. We had met at a mall in Portland to put a wish list together for their upcoming wedding, but they always seemed to be attracted to the silliest items that should never, ever make an appearance in a wedding registry. "That mini motorcycle is the stupidest thing on your already not stellar list. Pick something useful."

Caleb pushed the glasses up his nose and grinned. "But we don't need anything. We have all we need, really."

With a stunning smile, Sky pulled Caleb closer to his side and said, "We are all we need." They leaned their heads toward each other and kissed. My heart melted. I loved those two goofy, starry-eyed guys.

"Eww, come on, guys. Have some decorum," I said, my words belying how I felt. "So, so cheesy."

"Let's go to Cakes 'R' Us." In the four years since Sky had been reassigned as an earthbound angel and moved in with Caleb, he hadn't grown out of his passion for sugary treats. He ate sugar with such gusto you'd think he would be at least three hundred pounds, but he was as slim and muscular as he was the day they first met. One of the advantages of being an angel, he always said. "I'm in the mood for a Napoleon."

"You're always in the mood for decadent pastries," I said, threading my arm through the loop of his. "Let's go. It's getting chilly." Winter was over, snow had finally melted away, and spring flowers were trying to break through the still half-frozen ground of the state of Maine, also known as the Icicle State—well, by me, anyway.

I had finally graduated college, a semester ahead of schedule. I was not particularly smart or keen on schoolwork, but I was impatient since witnessing my parents lose their lives in a blink of an eye and my brother almost follow suit; I was in a hurry to live my life. I had quickly grown tired of the parties and excesses of college life and began taking extra classes to shrink the four years into something closer to three. I was finally free from the tight class schedule and the papers and exams. I could breathe now.

"So, what's this new job Caleb told me about?" Sky pulled me closer to him, knowing I was cold. He was never cold. Another advantage of being an angel, apparently. I had grown to love him and think of him as my brother, and I loved it when he could tell I needed a bit of warmth. "You're coming home finally?"

Home was in Wiscasset, a small and "quaint" town in Maine where my brother, with his youthful good looks, stuck out like a sore thumb. A town full of antique stores and fancy boutiques that seemed better suited to the older folk or the hip thirtysomething parents wanting to provide a small-town environment for their kids. I had lived there with my brother since my parents died and he became my legal guardian. When I moved into the college dorm, Sky and Caleb had the house to themselves, but they visited all the time. And I meant *all* the time. They would drive to Portland at least twice a month and take me to dinner because they "knew" I was not eating properly. Worse than parents.

"It's not in Wiscasset," I protested a bit too loudly. Caleb chuckled under his breath. "It's in Boothbay Harbor, and I've got my own apartment, not coming back to stay with the two of you lovebirds."

"Why not? You'd save a lot of money, and Boothbay is not that far," Caleb put in, obviously enjoying my discomfort with the whole idea of those two hovering over me like two mother hens.

"As if I really want to witness the two of you going at it like fucking rabbits." Caleb flinched. Even now he hated it when I cussed, which I often did to get a rise out of him. "No thank you. I have my own place closer to work."

"So, what is it anyway? What will you be doing?" Sky gave me another pull, the halo of his blond hair glowing in the sunlight.

"I'll be working for a local conservation group. I'll be studying the bay and saving whales."

"Really? Saving whales?"

Our lovely angel was seriously gullible sometimes.

I laughed as we ducked inside the bakery café. "No, silly. Not directly anyway. I won't even be able to save the lobsters. I'll be more of an errand girl." The scent of warm bread and sugary confections hit me, and I couldn't help a long, deep sniff. "Fuck! I've just gained five pounds with a whiff. There should be warning signs outside."

"Will you rein in your colorful language, girl? There are children here." My brother, twenty-nine going on eighty, gave me one of his stern looks. I shrugged and sat in a cozy booth in a corner.

We ordered some warm drinks and food—two shots of espresso for me, plus three pastries for Sky and one for Caleb and me to share. As much as I hated when my brother and his hot angel acted as if they were my parents, I also loved being around them. There was such love between those two that it made me yearn for my own love story. I hadn't much luck in the romance department. Most of my boyfriends so far had been total jerks who either wanted one thing and one thing only or were so needy I would have to give up on my life altogether to take care of them. No way in hell would I ever be willing to do that.

"I'm thinking of opening a small bakery café in Boothbay Harbor." It was a casual statement that I was hoping would go unnoticed, but Caleb's expression immediately destroyed that notion. "Don't look at me like that, brother. I can do it. I found a small place in the more residential, less touristy part of town that I can rent for a song. It needs a bit of work, but with your help, it'll look amazing in no time."

"But you'll be working. How are you going to find the time to invest in this venture?" Caleb, the skeptic.

Sky jumped to my defense. "She's an amazing baker, sweetheart. Her cookies are to die for." He smiled that little crooked smile of his. "Even the archangels love them." Yes, Gabriel was one of my cookies' biggest fans.

"Baking for your family is totally different than baking for business."

"Oh, ye of little faith," I quipped.

"And where are you going to get the money to rent the place and fix it up?"

"They are paying me good money and a generous stipend to help me with my rent," I said, taking a long sip of the hot coffee. "And I'm counting on my talented brother and his handyman to help me do all the fixing of the café for cheap."

Sky laughed. "Warning, angels are not handy around the house. There aren't that many pipes to fix or walls to paint in Arcadia."

I leaned over the table and held his hand. "Don't sell yourself short, my gorgeous angel of death." The memory of the dark angel I had seen a day or two before popped in my mind. "I forgot to tell you. I saw a dark angel a couple of days ago collecting a soul."

That sobered both of them up. "A dark angel? You didn't say anything, did you?" Caleb said, a panicky look in his eyes.

"Well, I did complain that he was too eager to take the man's soul even before the body was cold."

"You talked to him?" The smile died on Sky's lips. "You shouldn't have done that."

"Why? It's not as if he's going to take me away or anything," I protested. "Gabriel made sure that after what happened with Caleb, it wouldn't happen again to any human. What's the danger?"

Sky leaned over, his head almost touching mine over the table. "The danger is that you've alerted a dark angel about your gift to see them. Dark angels—any angel, really—don't like to be seen. It's against protocol. If a human can see through the charms we put in place every time we visit Earth, then something is wrong. Something that may require further examination."

I shrugged, pretending I was not a bit frazzled by his words. "So what? Let them investigate."

"Elfin, you do not want to have any of the dark lords looking into you, trust me. They're cruel and vicious angels who live to cause pain. Nothing gives them more pleasure than hurting a soul."

The conversation was giving me the shivers. "I'll be fine. They don't know who I am."

"You're coming home with us," Caleb said, his lips stretched into a line. "You may be in danger."

No way was I going to allow this to mess up my plans. "I'm going to Boothbay and that's that. I start working next week, I have to find myself a roommate, and I want to settle in first." I lifted a hand in front of his face. "Don't try to convince me otherwise. I know how to take care of myself."

I sounded more confident than I felt. Sky's words had me shaken. I still had nightmares about the time a dark angel had kidnapped my brother and taken him to the Dark Fortress, and when Sky had been tortured to within an inch of his life for pissing off the dark powers-that-be. I could handle a thief, but these angelic devils were something else completely.

They scared the shit out of me.

# CHAPTER 2

## COOKIES

## NIX

Human clothing was restrictive and scratchy, I thought. Dark angels didn't know much comfort, but our clothing allowed us all the movement we needed. Now, as I alit discreetly behind a building and shook my wings, I felt uncomfortable in what humans called a T-shirt and jeans. I didn't often retract my wings; there was rarely a need for it. Even when I slept, my wings were normally left unbound. With reluctance, I willed them to retract and listened to the quiet *whoosh* they made as they dwindled to nothing.

Still reeling from Asmodeus's orders to spy on the girl who had seen me a couple weeks ago, I began my short walk to where this human lived. I was not sure how my master found her, since I didn't even know her name, but I was about to officially meet the only human I knew who could see angels. In order to not bust my cover, Asmodeus had performed a special charm on me that would prevent her—or anyone else, including angels—from recognizing me.

I had been here in Boothbay Harbor often, plucking souls of men and women who had made poor choices during their lives. It was hard to understand how anyone who lived by the ocean could ever decide to do evil. The bright blue stretched as far as the eye could see in swells and dips, peaceful yet energetic. Yes, I had been here many times, but this was the first time I noticed the beauty of it all. For a moment I forgot who I was and what I was here to do as I gazed at the ocean, the seagulls barking over it and boats swaying in the gentle breeze. If only my life were that simple, that peaceful. I shook my head and resumed my walk.

The girl lived in an old house that had been converted into two apartments. Unused to walking in shoes, I tripped over a rock and almost fell face-first onto the steps of the house.

"A bit clumsy, aren't you?" I didn't have to look. I was certain I would recognize her voice anywhere—the tiny woman who had seen through the seraphic magic straight to my real self. I raised my head and met her gaze, two large brown eyes peering at me from the center of her face. "I'm pretty sure the step was already there."

I straightened myself and wiped my hands on my pants. "I'm not used to these shoes." What a lame thing to say, but I was a dark angel with no experience with humans.

She laughed and I felt the inside of my chest vibrate with the sound. "Then maybe you should buy a new pair, don't you think?"

She came down the steps to stand in front of me, not a hint of recognition on her face. Whatever my master had done, it'd worked. "I'm Joan. Who are you?"

Frozen for a second, I was stunned by a sudden realization—I couldn't remember my name. I must have had a name at some point, but I had no memories of anyone ever calling me anything other than a minion. I searched for ideas and spat out the first thing that came to my mind. "Phoenix. My name is Phoenix."

A smile spread along her full red lips. "Unusual, but I like it." She sat on the edge of the concrete wall that ran along the back of the steps. "Where did you come from?"

For a moment, I panicked. Had she recognized me? I didn't reply.

"Are you coming to reply to the ad?" I had no idea what she was talking about, but I nodded, unable to utter a word. "Let's go inside so I can give you the first degree." When I looked at her, confused, she laughed. "Damn, Phoenix, you have to grow a sense of humor. Let's go inside."

I followed her up the stairs and inside the house. Her upstairs apartment was small but radiated sunlight. It was a happy place, something I was not used to. I gasped in awe. "Did you hurt yourself?" she asked, misunderstanding the sound. I shook my head, still unable to say much.

Joan led me to a cozy living room, and we sat together on an old but comfortable white couch. She propped herself on a few cushions and curled her legs under her. "So, what makes you the perfect candidate to be my roommate?"

Roommate? What was that? And why would I want to be one? "Sorry, I—"

"Come on, don't sell yourself short. I'm in urgent need of a roommate. I can't afford this place by myself, and so far, all my candidates were idiots, both sexes included." She looked at me with hope in her eyes. "Well, do you want to share the apartment with me or not?"

Share the house with the person I was there to spy on? Perfect. "Yes, of course I do. What do I have to do?"

She smiled. "Tell me why I should take you. What can you do? Do you clean up after yourself? Are you tidy or have a tendency to hoard things?" Her eyes turned into round orbs. "And please don't tell me you have a cat. They're cute, but I'm allergic to them."

I swallowed before answering, "No cats. I'm tidy, and I'd be glad to clean the house for you." I had done a lot worse for Asmodeus. Cleaning sounded like a vacation to me.

"Do you have a job in town?" she asked, curiosity shining in her eyes. "How will you pay for the rent? I need a roommate that can actually pay the rent." She giggled softly.

An angel in the Department of Intelligence had prepared me for this question. "I'm independently wealthy," I repeated the well-rehearsed words. "A family inheritance."

Joan squinted, and for a moment I thought she wouldn't believe me, but then she said, "Wow, that's fucking awesome. I can't even imagine not having to worry about finances."

We talked for a couple hours, Joan asking all kinds of questions and me trying my best to answer them without giving away who I really was. In the end, her fine-boned face lit up and she jumped to her knees, holding one of the cushions against her chest. "You're fucking perfect. An angel in disguise." I must have cringed because she added, "What I'm saying is you have the place. When can you move in?"

"Today?" Was that too early?

"Deal." She stretched her hand out to me. "Let's shake on it." We did, and I found that I liked the warmth of her hand against my palm. "Do you need help bringing your stuff in?"

Shit! I had no stuff. None at all. "I left all of my things back where I lived." She arched a brow. "Long story. I'll have to buy a few things."

Joan threw the cushion up in the air and hooted. "My favorite words: buy things. Give me a couple hours to go tend to some things and I will take you shopping. What do you say?"

I nodded, slightly overwhelmed by her enthusiasm. "What do I do until then?" I had no place to go or anything to do.

"Hang around here, watch some TV, eat some cookies." She pointed at the narrow kitchen. "I baked them myself. Take a nap. I'll be back as soon as I can."

Before I knew it, she left in a whirlwind of activity as she picked up her backpack and slipped into the shoes she had kicked off on her way in. I was alone, and the silence seemed oppressive now that her bubbly voice was gone. I grabbed one of the cushions and hugged it. Not sure how it happened, but I was now living under the same roof with the human I had been sent to investigate. Asmodeus would be impressed. Then again, he wouldn't. Nothing impressed my master. He couldn't care less how I did it as long as I did exactly what he told me to do. I was nothing but a minion for the cruelest overlord in the Fortress, and he made sure to remind me every chance he got.

I looked around, suddenly overwhelmed with it all. The spot I called home was nothing more than a hovel, a small hole in the viscous wall of the Fortress. My only possession was a thin blanket that I crawled under at night on the hard floor to close my eyes for a few hours. Angels didn't need a lot of sleep, but I enjoyed the relative peace of slumber. I had somehow learned how to block out thoughts and dreams, and my sleep was normally a blank space in time where this dark world I was a part of didn't exist. Joan's apartment was small but airy and bright. I let the word home roll around in my mouth until it felt familiar and then decided to explore it.

The windows in the living room faced the street, where life outside was unaware that an angel of evil was taking up residence. Cars drove by slowly, and people walked up and down the slightly slanted sidewalk, chatting, talking on the phone, some strolling, some rushing. I watched, fascinated. I had never really paid much attention to the human world. I came, plucked, and left. There was not much point in studying creatures who would sooner or later die with their souls to either be plucked or collected, depending on the choices they had made in life. But standing there, staring out the window and in no hurry to do anything, I was seized by a curiosity I had never experienced. How would it feel to be a human? What did these mortals do all day? Joan had mentioned work. Was her work anything like what I did? Did she have a master who told her what to do and punished her when she didn't do it properly?

"I know very little about humans," I whispered to no one in particular. Catching sight of my reflection in the window, I cringed. Was that how I looked? Asmodeus was right; I didn't look any different from the other humans when my wings were hidden and my body was covered in mortal clothes. I brushed a hand over my short, thick hair and was startled by the eyes staring back at me. My mind might be numb, but my eyes told a different story—haunted like the eyes of the souls I had plucked through the years.

⸸

## JOAN

"This coffee sucks," I said, spitting a mouthful of the horrible brown liquid back into the mug where it'd come from. We had met for a cup in a coffee shop by the harbor.

"It's not that bad," Tess said, gulping down the brew as if tasting the most delicious thing in the world. "Better than the coffee on campus."

Tess was my best friend. We had met in high school when she still lived in Wiscasset, and we'd continued our friendship after we went to different colleges. We graduated at the same time a few months back, even though she started school a year earlier than me.

"I was in no hurry, unlike you, munchkin," she would say, knowing all too well I hated being called that. I was pretty short, but so what? I preferred to think I was fun-sized, like Hershey's chocolates or the tiny pastries they sold in European patisseries.

"It's hell in a cup." I liked hyperboles when I needed to emphasize something, a fact that had made most of my English teachers frown. "This town seriously needs our help, Tess."

"But I'm hopeless in the kitchen. You know that, Jojo." She was terrible. In fact, she lived on sandwiches and canned soup whenever she couldn't eat out.

"I don't need you in the kitchen," I said, pushing the offending coffee away from me. "I need you to manage the café while I'm in charge of the baking. I'll bake, and you make sure the customers get and pay for what they want."

"Are you going to put me in one of those ruffled aprons?"

I laughed at the image in my mind—Tess, with her short, spiky hair and many piercings and tattoos in a ruffled tiny apron. "I don't think so. I don't want to scare the customers."

"I can be dainty," Tess protested, sticking her pinky out as she brought the mug to her lips again. "See?"

"Right. Really dainty." I snorted. "I want you to be yourself and nobody else. Do you think you can handle that?"

Tess pretended to give it a thought. "Do I have to brew the coffee too?"

"Fuck no. If you think this is good coffee, I can only imagine what you'd brew." I smiled at my best friend, already imagining her working with me in my dream bakery café. "It's going to be great."

Tess took another swig and wiped her mouth with the back of her hand. "So, when will this place open?"

"Caleb and Sky are going to help me set it up," I said, taking a glance at my phone. "Shit. How long have I been here?"

"A couple of hours. Why?"

"I left my new roommate at the house." I hopped to my feet, feeling guilty I had taken so long. "I've got to go. Tess, come and see me tomorrow if you can. Let's talk some more."

"Who's this roommate? Is she hot?"

I was already halfway to the door. I waved and yelled back, "She's a he, Tess. Nothing you'd be interested in." She laughed as I opened the front door and left.

It wasn't bad enough that I left a stranger sitting in my living room alone, but I had left him there for over two hours. By now he'd either taken off with my flat-screen TV or left, never to return. I thanked myself for having worn my comfy sneakers and ran all the way up the hill from the harbor to the block where I lived. I loved my tiny house, which was technically an apartment. The owners had split the house into two levels; the lower level was a garage turned studio apartment, and the upper was the house proper where I lived. My neighbor, an old lady with a cute dog, lived in the converted garage.

I flew up the steps and through the door and was pleased to see Phoenix still sitting where I left him, his head resting on the back of the couch and eyes closed. Had he moved at all? He didn't seem to notice my clumsy entrance, and I stole the moment to study him more carefully. He was hot as lava, dark and broody, with eyes sheltered by thick, dark lashes and eyebrows. His olive-skinned face was covered in a light scruff the same color as his dark brown hair. I had never met him before today, and yet he looked oddly familiar.

"Are you sleeping?" I asked finally. His eyes popped open, and for a moment he seemed lost and confused. "Sorry I took so long."

Phoenix glanced at me, and I was stunned by what I saw in his eyes. How had I missed it earlier? There was a poignant, tormented cloud over his gorgeous hazel eyes, hauntingly beautiful in its sadness. "It's okay. I took a nap."

"Good. I'll make some coffee, and then we can sit and talk terms of our agreement." I dropped my backpack on a chair and stole a glance at him. "Where are you from?"

He hesitated. "What do you mean?"

What else could I possibly mean? Wasn't the question self-explanatory?

"Where did you live before?" I dug a couple of coffee pods from the cabinet and began brewing it. I was picky about my coffee, so I bought nothing but the best, the only thing I splurged on. "Or do you live in town?"

I heard the sound of shuffling, and his face appeared at the door to the kitchen. "I just arrived here," he said, his body filling the opening completely. He was tall, with wide shoulders and arms that bulged from the sleeves of his black T-shirt. I waited for him to tell me where he was from, but he offered no information. "Have you lived here long?"

I plopped another pod in the machine and handed him the first mug and a spoon. "There's sugar and creamer on the table," I told him, waving at my bistro set in a corner of the small kitchen. "I've only just moved here too. I finished college a couple months ago and got a job here."

Phoenix sat in one of the two chairs by the table and began stirring his coffee even though he had not helped himself to any sugar or cream. "I like your house. It has a lot of light."

Joining him at the table, I poured two spoonfuls of sugar and an individual container of creamer into my coffee. "Thank you. Have you seen the rooms?"

He shook his head. "Only the living room and the kitchen." He smelled the coffee and wrinkled his nose.

"You don't like coffee?" It was almost as if he was afraid of it.

He licked his lips and looked at me. "I've never drank it."

"What? No fucking way!" I didn't know a single person who had never tasted coffee. Even Sky had become a java drinker, though his taste for the brew was questionable at best. "How is that possible?"

With another of his bewildered looks, he shrugged. "There's not much of it where I come from."

"Tarnation." I still used Sky's old-fashioned expression a lot. "Where the fuck did you come from? Hell?"

Was I imagining it, or had he blanched? "No, a small town in rural Iowa." He winced a little, as if his words tasted sour.

I laughed. "Dude, you really need to grow a sense of humor.

I was joking." Did he ever smile? Such a handsome face but permanently stuck in a bleak expression.

As if making a sudden decision, he put the mug to his lips and took a sip. If possible, he looked even more confused. He took another sip and wrinkled his perfect nose again. "Strange flavor," he said. "Not unpleasant."

"Where have you been all your life? Coffee is the chosen drink of the gods. Hot and delicious." I thought of coffee as a friend. "It's liquid heaven."

"No such thing," he said, grimacing.

"Trust me on this, dude. Coffee is liquid goodness." I stood up and went to fetch a plate of cookies I had on the counter. "Here, eat a cookie. You look hungry."

Phoenix stared at the chocolate chip cookies as if he were seeing an alien. "What are those?"

"Now you are shitting me, right?" He didn't seem to be joking though. "Cookies. Chocolate chip cookies. I made them myself. Take one."

Hesitantly, he picked one up and sniffed it. I giggled and urged him to try a bite by taking one myself. He raised the cookie to his lips, took a tiny bite, and something amazing happened; his eyes began to shine and his face opened into a stunning smile.

So, Phoenix could smile after all.

# CHAPTER 3

## ROOMMATES

## NIX

I couldn't get enough of these delicious morsels my human charge called cookies. As an angel, I rarely had to eat, and food at the Fortress was not exactly tasty, but as soon as I took a bite of the round, brown confection, it was as if my taste buds exploded. My lips stretched into an unfamiliar shape that I belatedly recognized as a smile. I couldn't remember ever smiling. Certainly, I must have done it at some point, but that memory was buried like so many others inside the fog that was my past.

"So, I guess you like them." Tiny Joan stared at me, sitting at the edge of her seat, a silly smile on her lips.

I nodded, reluctant to let her know how much I liked them. I wasn't here to make friends with her. Just the opposite. But I was dying to take another bite. Instead, I slipped the cookie into my pocket to eat it later.

"What do I need to do? Sign a contract or something?" I went back to what I hoped was a businesslike voice. Asmodeus had ordered me to watch a few human TV shows to get acquainted with mortal ways. I had practiced for days, but I still felt uncomfortable, and I was quite sure it came across clearly to anyone listening to me.

Joan sat back and slapped her hands on the seat cushion. "Well, back to business, I guess. Yes, I have a simple contract for you to sign. Basically, it states that you are responsible to reimburse me for any damage you cause and that if you are to bring any girl or boyfriends here, you'll be respectful of my space and peace and quiet. In other words, no walking around naked or having sex on the couch."

I had no intention of having anyone over. In fact, when was the last time I'd had sex? Consensual sex? Another thing I had no memory of. It wasn't as if angels didn't have sex, but I had never had a choice in the matter. Sex for me spelled nothing but violence and cruelty.

"It's a deal. Where do I sign?"

My room was small but full of light, with windows facing the harbor. The house was on the side of a hill, which meant I could see the sparkling blue waters of the bay over the roofs of the other houses. I was shocked how much that sight affected me. Looking at the spread of calm waters sprinkled with boats and fishing buoys brought me a sense of peace, a feeling I seemed to remember but couldn't think of why or when.

I sighed so loudly, Joan threw me a curious glance. "Do you like it?" she asked.

This time I didn't stop myself in time and told her the truth. "Yes, the view is beautiful." The word beautiful sounded foreign to my ears, and I must have cringed because she gave me another weird look. "Totally adequate."

My new roommate chuckled as if I had told a joke. "You use the weirdest expressions," she said. What did she mean? "You remind me of my brother's fiancé and how he used to use the strangest words."

That statement offered me an out of this awkward conversation. "Does he live close? Your brother?"

"Not too far," she said, opening a drawer of the dresser and storing a pile of towels. "A short drive from here. He comes to visit often, the lovable idiot. He thinks he's my father." She laughed and closed the drawer. "If you run out of towels, it's your own fault. The washer and dryer are in the small storage room off the kitchen. Use it often."

With those words, she left me alone in the room, still a bit dazed by the feelings the gorgeous sight was stirring inside of me. It was as if the waters were calling, a song that echoed inside of me and pulled at strings I didn't even know existed. I had seen this harbor before since I had plucked many souls from this area, but I supposed I never paid much attention to it. Or maybe the fact that I was focused on my job had clouded my perception. I stood by the window for a long time, watching and longing for something I couldn't name. It was both pleasant and horribly painful, a mixture of joy and sadness.

When I left the room later, still wearing the same clothes—the only ones I brought with me—Joan was sitting at the kitchen table, munching on her delicious cookies, and I was suddenly reminded of the one I had sneaked inside my pocket. It was most likely in crumbles by now, but I had every intention of indulging later. I only wished I had thought of taking it out and leaving it somewhere safe in the room.

"You said you'd take me shopping for clothes," I told her, wistfully gazing at the treats she was eating. "Where can I do it?"

She stopped her hand halfway to her mouth and arched her eyebrows. "At a store, of course. Your hometown must be a desolate place. Don't you have stores there?"

I gulped. Damn. I was showing my lack of human knowledge again. I frantically searched my recollections of what I had watched on TV for a point of reference. "I meant, what store do you recommend?"

That seemed to satisfy her, and she resumed her eating. "Are you looking for cheap or stylish?"

I couldn't care less and actually had no idea what both of those things really meant. "I don't care. All I want is a replacement for the ones I'm wearing."

She gave me a once-over, her eyes roaming over my faded old jeans and black T-shirt. "You could use a little help," she mumbled under her breath. "Dude, that style hasn't been a style in over a generation." What style was she referring to? "Yes, I'll take you shopping. You need all the help you can get. Unless you prefer my brother to do it."

The idea of another mortal helping me was almost unbearable at that moment. Pretending I was something I wasn't was exhausting. "No, that's all right. You can take me. Thank you for offering. I don't know much about clothes."

Joan rolled her eyes and huffed. "Obviously." Something told me I should be offended. "Let's go, Captain Obvious. Let's make you look like you belong in this decade."

## JOAN

For such a hot guy, Phoenix sure had no style whatsoever. His jeans were so dated, archaeologists and historians would have a field day with them. I took him downtown and showed him around several clothing stores, where he proceeded to pick the first thing he saw, with no concept of color or size. I was pretty sure if I hadn't been there, he would have left the store dressed like a clown or a pilgrim.

"Are you ready, Nix?" I asked, sitting impatiently outside the dressing room where he was trying on some clothes I'd picked out for him.

"Who's Nix?" he asked, sliding the curtain open.

I almost choked on the gum I was chewing. Phoenix had been good-looking in the clothes he was wearing. He was absolutely stunning in the ones he wore now.

"What?" I asked, finding it hard to talk. His olive complexion stood out in all its glory against the cream sweater I'd chosen, and the dark blue jeans he was wearing accentuated the muscles of his upper thighs.

"Nix. Who's Nix?" he asked again, his dark eyebrows arching over his amazing hazel eyes—the color of green olives, if olives could actually shine.

I struggled to compose myself and cleared my throat. "You. Nix, short for Phoenix." I couldn't take my eyes off him. And I tried, I swear I tried, but my treacherous eyeballs kept roving over his tall, delicious body while my mind was totally undressing him. *Oh, be still, my naughty bits!*

He stopped for a moment, lost in thought. "But that's not my name," he said, looking positively puzzled.

I sighed again, incapable of controlling myself any longer. "I know that, Phoenix. It's a nickname. People use them all the time." Seriously, where had he come from? "If you really hate it, I won't call you that."

He shook his head and licked his luscious lips. "I don't mind. I like it." I almost burst out laughing when he added, "I give you permission to call me Nix."

Who talked like that? Funny, sexy Phoenix apparently did. Sky could be related to him for all I knew. They both talked awkwardly and in old-fashioned ways and seemed surprised by the most everyday things. But where Phoenix was dark and moody, Sky was bright and open.

"How does it look?" he asked. "Does it meet with your approval?"

Did it ever! I nodded instead of talking. My voice caught in my throat, right next to the knot formed by my desire to grab him and kiss him.

"Let's buy it, then," he said, striding toward the register without bothering to change back into his jeans and T-shirt.

I stopped him by grabbing his arm. Holy shit! My hand hardly fit around his hard bicep. I gulped. "No, not yet, dude. You need at least one more outfit." A thought hit me. "Are you strapped for money? I can lend you some." And then ask my brother to cover it. I hadn't been paid yet and already had to cover the rent for both the apartment and the store space for the café.

"I've got plenty of money, but thank you for offering." He looked back at the dressing room, where a couple other outfits I had picked for him still hung from the hangers and frowned. "Do I have to try them all?"

I had to laugh. Such a male thing to ask. "Of course. How else are you going to know whether they fit you and look good?"

His eyes narrowed as he furrowed his forehead. "Is it that important they look good?"

Well, he could walk around naked and I was sure no one would mind, because if he looked that good with clothes, I could only imagine—and I did—how he'd look without them. But unfortunately, we lived in the real world where people—even hotties like Phoenix—needed to cover their bodies.

"Yes, it is. Or you'll never get yourself a girlfriend." Not true. He could wear a plain potato sack and still have women flutter around him like moths to a flame. "That is if you like girls. Or do you prefer men?"

He looked puzzled. "Does it matter?" Oh my God, what was his deal? Of course it mattered. I wanted to know. "I never thought about it." What?

"You don't know whether you're gay or straight?" Now I was the one confused. How could he not know?

"I have no preference, I mean. I'm not looking for a relationship anyway."

"Who said anything about a relationship? What about getting laid once in a while?" My brother would have given me the look of death if he heard me say those words. At least I hadn't said "fuck." That showed improvement, right?

"What's that? Getting laid."

I threw my arms up in the air in surrender. Either he was excellent at pretending or he had rolled out from under a rock somewhere in the universe, possibly another planet. "Okay, forget it. Just try the fucking clothes."

Soon after, we left the store, leaving his old clothes in the trash. Carrying the two bags with the new outfits in one hand, Phoenix looked like a god. Stubble covered his chin and cheeks, and he seemed perfectly oblivious to the many admiring looks he attracted as we walked along the streets of Boothbay Harbor. I tried to get him to stop at another store to get a coat, but he dismissed the idea, claiming he never got cold. Whatever! Weirdo, that's what he was—a hot-as-hell weirdo.

"I have to stop at Hannaford's. Do you want to come with me

or go home?" I asked him.

"I'll go with you." There was no hesitation this time. I guess I hadn't totally spooked him yet.

We crossed the road in the direction of the supermarket, halfway to my house. I was planning on baking like a crazed woman to start the marketing campaign for my business, and I needed a lot of supplies. I felt stupidly pleased that a stranger I had just met was willing to come along, so I was sure I was smiling like a fool as we approached the store.

Phoenix, who had been quiet for a while, turned to me as we went around the street corner and asked, "What's a Hannaford?"

## NIX

For a moment I forgot who I was and what I was supposed to be doing. My eyes couldn't believe the number of choices humans had for food products. As far as I could remember, I had eaten one thing and one thing only—the goop that went for nutrition at the Fortress. I had seen Asmodeus eating things that were not available to any of us lowly angels, but this was mind-blowing. Row after row, shelves upon shelves stuffed with all kinds of food in all shapes and sizes. I followed my human along the narrow corridors between shelves in a state of wonderment as I watched other mortals pack their carts with products.

"Do you really plan on eating all of this?" I asked, staring at Joan's cart that she had piled high with bags of flour, sugar, sprinkles—

was that edible?—and those delicious things called chocolate chips.

She giggled, stretching her arms up to a box on the top shelf. Even on her tiptoes, she couldn't reach it. I reached over and grabbed the package for her, adding it to the cart. "Not all of it. I'll be baking lots of cookies to give away to promote my new business."

"What business is that?"

"I'm opening a bakery café as soon as I get the place fixed." She held on to the cart's handle and pushed it toward the front of the store. "Do you want to help?"

Puzzled by the question, I tilted my head and asked, "With what? Eating the cookies?" That idea was pleasing indeed. I was looking forward to eating the smashed confection I had rescued from the pocket of my old pants and was now hiding inside the bag with the new clothes. Eating more of those heavenly morsels would definitely please me.

Surprisingly, Joan burst out laughing and almost hit her forehead on the cart. "You're too funny, Nix." I wasn't trying to be. "No, helping me fix the place. My brother and his boyfriend are going to help, but they are busy with their own lives and won't be able to come any time soon." She stopped laughing and wiped a tear from her eye. "I would be, however, willing to provide you with as many cookies as you can eat as payment."

It was hard to tell whether she was serious, and I had no idea what helping her "fix the place" actually entailed, but if doing it would keep me close to her at all times, I was willing to give it a try. I nodded and was rewarded with a smile. She had an interesting face, like those on the girls in paintings by Vermeer, only darker.

I stopped abruptly—where had that come from? What did I know about anyone's paintings? Had I ever plucked souls from art museums? I couldn't recall it but could clearly see those female faces, pale and serene, illuminated by the soft light that seeped through windows.

Joan stopped and glanced at me, her forehead furrowed. "Are you okay? You went pale all of a sudden."

My breathing had sped up as if I couldn't take enough oxygen in. Considering angels could go a long time without breathing, this was worrisome. "I'm fine. Just had a surprising thought."

"A good or bad one?" She resumed her walking, pushing the cart ahead. "You looked stunned."

I shook my head, trying to calm myself down. I had probably seen the paintings on some TV show before heading to Earth. "Nothing important. It was unexpected, that's all."

Joan paid for the groceries at what she called a register, and then we both stepped out into the cool air, hands full of bags burgeoning with food. The apartment was not too far, only a few streets up from there, but my fingers were numb from holding on to the thin straps of the bags. "Do you normally do this alone?" I asked. How could such a tiny person carry all that by herself?

She opened her mouth and eyes into almost perfect circles. "I work out," she said as if that answered my question. "There is well-toned muscle under these sleeves."

"You're a pretty small woman."

"So small women can't be strong? What a sexist thing to say, Nix. I'm shocked." She didn't look shocked. There was definitely a tiny smile on the corner of her lips and a twinkle in her eye. I had only just met her but was quickly learning how to read her body language.

I chose to be quiet for fear of saying the wrong thing. She opened the front door, and we both went directly to the small kitchen to deposit the bags on the counter. I left her to it and went to store my new purchases in the closet and dresser in my room. Joan had insisted I buy underwear, something I'd never worn, and some toiletries I didn't need. As an angel, I had no need for toothbrush, deodorant, or even soap, but apparently humans did, so I opted to do what she suggested.

As soon as I was done putting everything away, I pulled out the cookie—now mostly crumbs—and sat on the edge of the bed to eat it. I closed my eyes and enjoyed the sweetness on my tongue and the grainy texture that melted into nectar in my mouth. I had heard of heaven, had even encountered some angels of light, but I now understood why so many humans strove to go to heaven, if it was anything like this—what had Joan called it?—chocolate chip cookie.

## JOAN

"Holy shit, Jojo. You've been holding out on me." Tess had that look that told me she was about to act totally embarrassing.

"Don't you dare say anything," I warned her, a finger stuck in her direction. I glanced at Phoenix, who was studying a rolling pin with a puzzled expression.

"You didn't tell me he was hot."

I shushed her. "He'll hear you." I glanced at him again, but he didn't seem to have heard anything. "What do you care anyway? It's not like you like guys."

"That doesn't mean I can't tell when I'm in the presence of a fine specimen of the male sex." She looked over my head. "Hey, Phoenix!"

I tried to stop her, but it was too late. My handsome roommate saw Tess waving at him and walked over.

Tess gave me a triumphant look. "Fuck you, Tess." I loved her, but she could be such a pain sometimes.

Phoenix still had the rolling pin in his hand. "What's this? Some kind of weapon?"

Tess burst out laughing. "This dude is hilarious."

I had a feeling he wasn't joking, so I smiled at him. "No, a rolling pin." He stared at the kitchen tool, confused. "To roll out dough."

"Hah, interesting," he muttered, placing the object on the table. "Who are you?"

Tess offered him her hand. "Tess Holden. I'm Joan's bestie." Phoenix shook her hand awkwardly. "Nice to meet you."

"Likewise," Phoenix said before leaning over and whispering to me, "What's a bestie?"

I shook my head, still not quite used to my roommate's quirkiness. "Tess is my best friend," I explained. "We've been friends since we were little."

Tess was still staring at him, a wicked smile on her face. "Where's your girlfriend?" I should kill her. No judge on this land would convict me.

Phoenix arched his brow. "No girlfriend. What are we doing here, Joan?"

It had been almost a month since I met Phoenix, and we had come down to the bakery to start working on it. "I thought that maybe we could at least start stripping the walls of the horrible old paper. Tess came to help. Didn't you, Tess?"

My friend made a big production of rolling her sleeves, revealing part of her arm tattoos. "Sure."

I had to show Phoenix what to do, but once he figured it out, he worked quietly and efficiently, stripping the paper faster than Tess and I together, not once stopping to rest. Eventually I told him to take a break—he may not be tired, but I was. My arms ached from stretching over my head, and my fingers were numb from scraping the bits of stubborn paper.

We all sat at an old rickety table and chairs that was left by the former owner. I brought some cookies and hot coffee that I poured for the three of us. Phoenix smelled the brew and drank it whole in a few gulps. After the first time, he had taken a liking to coffee and drank it every time I offered but never asked for it on his own. In fact, he never asked for anything. Unless it was offered, he was content with what he had. I sometimes wondered if he would even eat a meal if I didn't cook it and invite him to partake.

"So, Phoenix." Uh-oh, Tess was on the prowl. "Jojo tells me

you're from Iowa."

He blinked his intense hazel eyes momentarily before replying, "Yes." Phoenix was also seriously thrifty with words.

"Where at?" Tess didn't give up easily. I threw her a "quit it" look, but she ignored me.

"You wouldn't recognize it. It's in the middle of nowhere," my roommate said, stuffing his mouth with the cookie.

"Oh, come on, tell me."

Phoenix looked at her for a moment, no hint of a smile on his face. "Beaconsfield." That was new information for me too. I couldn't wait to google it. "Tiny town."

Tess smiled and opened her eyes at me, obviously pleased with herself. "How come you're here now?"

"No jobs back home." He hadn't even raised his eyes this time, his focus totally on the cookie in his hand.

"You don't talk much, do you?" Tess's slightly irritated voice made me smile. She was trying to squeeze blood from a stone.

Phoenix didn't bother to answer, just shrugged. "This is good," he said, looking at me. He had a smattering of cookie crumbs in the corner of his lips, and before I could stop myself, I reached out and wiped it clean with my finger.

Big mistake. Huge. I swear I felt electricity run through me, starting on my index finger and rushing through my whole body to parts of me I didn't want too excited at that time of day. He must have felt it too, because his eyes opened wide and locked with mine for a fleeting moment. The world stopped turning for an instant, and everything around us ceased to exist.

Until Tess brought me down from my reverie. "Hello. Come back to Earth, my friend."

I moved my gaze away from his and blinked a few times. "What?"

Tess giggled. "You got it bad," she whispered, and my face caught on fire. Then louder she asked, "What are you going to name the bakery?"

With my breath back to normal-ish, I avoided looking in Phoenix's direction for fear of my own thoughts. "I think I have a name. What do you think about Heavenly Cookies?"

Both Tess and I turned to Phoenix, who had started to cough uncontrollably as if he was choking on something. Tess stood up and moved behind his chair to pat him on the back. I stifled a chuckle. It looked like she was trying to burp him. "Are you okay, Nix?" I asked instead.

He couldn't answer, fits of coughing still exploding out of him. I went to fetch a glass of water and offered it to him. "Here, drink some water."

After a while the cough subsided, but his face was red and his eyes were wet with tears. "What was that?" he asked, his voice hoarse from all the hacking.

I laughed. "You choked on the cookie, I guess." I handed him another glass of water. "Drink some more. I'll make you some warm tea to soothe your throat."

I filled the mug with water and placed it in the small microwave on the counter to heat it up. A prickling on my neck made me turn around to find my handsome roommate's eyes on me. A lovely shiver rippled through me, and I fully expected him to lower his eyes like he normally did. But not this time. Unlike before, Phoenix held my gaze for longer than I expected. There was a sadness in the depths of his eyes that contradicted his quirkiness and lack of social graces. I wondered what kind of secrets those reflective pools were hiding.

By the time we were finished, it was already getting dark. Tess jumped on her motorcycle and waved us goodbye as she disappeared around the corner.

Phoenix and I walked side by side, mere shadows on the walls as we passed under dim streetlights, at first quiet. "Do you have any family?" I asked as we headed the few blocks over for home. I was constantly mentioning my brother, but he never talked about anyone at all. Not even a friend.

"No family." It was said with indifference. Maybe he had never met his family? Maybe they were all dead?

"What about friends? Did you leave any friends behind in Iowa?"

"No friends either." His soft voice echoed in the dark, melodious but somewhat grim. "No such thing where I come from."

His last statement made me shiver. What did he mean by that? We continued on our way in silence, but at one point I could have sworn I had seen wings on his shadow on the wall.

# CHAPTER 4
## TRAUMAS

## NIX

Almost two months had passed since I arrived at her door. I had half expected she would want me gone by now, considering I knew nothing of human habits and was quite useless as a human myself. However, Joan seemed happy to have me around. The strange, tiny woman went about her life with a permanent smile on her face, always busy, always coming up with new ideas for things to do. I didn't understand most of what she said, but she was always ready to explain it to me. With each passing day, I felt more familiar with life around me, and I caught myself dangerously forgetting the reason I was there.

Asmodeus had kept silent all this time, and I began wondering whether he had forgotten about me. I wouldn't mind. Even though I was a fish out of water among the mortals, life with them was a huge improvement from the one I led at the Fortress. I came and went as I pleased, lived in comfort, and of course, there were cookies. And in all honesty, I enjoyed Joan's company too.

After watching her closely for the past few weeks, I hadn't discovered anything unusual about her. I would often catch her watching me when she thought I wasn't aware, but she hadn't shown any signs of recognition. Not that I expected it. Asmodeus had done his special kind of voodoo on me so she wouldn't, but I was glad for a different reason; I'd hate if she remembered me not as her awkward and friendly roommate but as the dark angel plucking souls from those who passed. It had never bothered me before, but now the idea of her thinking ill of me was unbearable. I didn't quite understand it, but I wanted her to think of me as a good person.

Her bakery space was nearing completion, at least aesthetically. The walls had been stripped and painted, the counters and cabinets sanded and stained, and a refurbished granite countertop installed by one of Tess's friends. Joan's brother had promised to come the next weekend and help build the cookie stands and shop for a fridge. I was doing my share, even though I wasn't sure I was doing it right. Joan kept assuring me I was doing a great job, but I suspected she was just being nice. I had never met anyone as generous as she was. Her friends were indeed fortunate to have her, someone always willing to lend a hand, no questions asked.

"Get dressed." Joan jumped off her perch on the couch and waved at me. I looked at her, puzzled. "I'm taking you somewhere. Come on, go put on some warmer clothes." I found I loved walking around in what Joan called loungers and a T-shirt. It was the closest to my angel clothes, which were minimal and threadbare.

"Why?" Joan didn't believe me when I told her I didn't get cold. Angels never did.

"Will you stop asking fucking questions and hurry?"

Joan had a colorful vocabulary, or so she said. I couldn't tell. It seemed to me she talked like everyone else, but she assured me her brother was always on her case for having a filthy mouth. I made her laugh when I told her I had checked and there was nothing dirty about her mouth. I was not kidding.

After layering a hoodie over my black T-shirt and slipping into some athletic shoes, I followed her down to the harbor as she enthusiastically chatted away. I wasn't listening to her words but to her voice instead; it was soothing even when she shouted. I guessed it was like music to a lot of humans.

I was so distracted by the harmonious tones of her voice that I didn't notice we were in the harbor, standing on one of the quays. "What are we going to do? Jump in the water?" Which I knew was still freezing this time of the year.

She laughed again. "No, idiot. I'm taking you on a short excursion of the bay." She waved at a man on a boat, who waved back. "You don't get seasick, do you?"

I had no idea since I'd never been on a boat long enough to find out. Plucking souls from sea vessels didn't take long. I shrugged noncommittally.

We both boarded the small boat, the wind blowing waves

against its sides and rocking it so hard I almost lost my footing. Without my wings, my balance was not at its best, it seemed.

The captain moved us away from the quay, his weathered skin almost the color of the wood trim along the boat. "Nice day for a quick sail," he commented, never taking his eyes away from the waters ahead. The briny scent of the ocean's waters hit me full force even though we were still some ways from it, a strong, pleasantly fresh odor that made me inhale deeply. My lungs liked it and wanted more. Seagulls cawed their strange songs above us, and the few passengers on some of the touring boats were leaning over the sides, enjoying the cool, fresh air of the harbor.

"We've been working so hard lately, I thought we deserved a break," Joan said, her voice barely audible over the humming of the wind and the roar of the motor. "I'm taking you to my special place, but you have to swear you'll never tell anyone where it is."

I nodded despite my confusion. Why would I tell anyone? Anyone besides Asmodeus, that was. Not that he would be interested in her comings and goings outside the fact that she could see angels even through our charms. Not sure anymore if I wanted to give my master any information about my roommate, I did, however, want to find out why she had been able to see me that day. In all my years as a dark angel, I had never been seen by a mortal.

Not a half hour later, the boat docked on an old, decrepit slip near what looked like a tiny island. There didn't seem to be much to it—some trees, a house or two, and little more. The sailor helped us step off the vessel but made no move to follow us.

"Isn't he coming with us?"

"No, Jeb will stay here and wait for us to return. There isn't much to do on this island anyway."

Then why were we there?

I followed her up a beaten path framed by the kind of dry grasses that seemed to thrive in sandy lands until we were on the top of the short hill. As soon as she got there, a few steps ahead of me, Joan opened her arms wide and yelled from the top of her lungs. No words, only sounds. I was surprised by the primal tone of her cry, as if she were an animal out in the wild.

Two more steps and I joined her. What I saw stunned me into complete silence. The view from up there was overwhelmingly beautiful. The other side of the tiny island was greener with both low and tall grasses growing together in harmony, an abandoned-looking cottage with a white roof at the bottom where a white sandy beach met the blue waters of the bay. The sky, bluer than it had been in a long while, seemed to be blessing us with a kind of intrinsic joy that defied reason. Inside my chest, a funny feeling, like the fluttering of a thousand butterfly wings, grew—a feeling I couldn't identify at first; it was as unfamiliar as it was welcomed.

"Do you feel it? A tickle in your gut, a sudden wish to fly?" Joan asked, her arms still spread, eyes closed, and nose up, inhaling the air. "Happiness. Pure happiness."

Was that what I was feeling? Joy? Was it possible? I'd heard about it but never felt it. There was no joy in the Fortress, no moments of beauty and light. Dark and gloom were all that existed, with no expectations of sunshine or laughter. The Fortress was sadness, agony. I liked the new feeling swelling inside of me, so I closed my eyes to fully enjoy it.

As quickly as it came, the wave of joy suddenly turned into an oily cloud of darkness. My eyes snapped open.

"What the fuck are you doing, minion?" Asmodeus's voice shook me to the core. From the sense of flying without actually leaving the ground, I went straight to despair, the darkness that always seeped into my soul whenever I was around my master. "I did not send you to Earth to have fun. You're supposed to be watching this human and learning why she can see angels."

I stole a glance in her direction, but she didn't seem to have heard anything. The dark master was speaking directly into my head. Could I reply the same way?

"Yes, idiot. You can talk to me with your thoughts. Spill the beans."

I gulped. What could I say? "I have been watching her, Asmodeus, but she seems to be a normal human. I haven't witnessed anything that would explain why she saw me plucking that soul."

"Are you following her everywhere? Hovering over her when she sleeps and haunting her dreams?"

I didn't even know I could do that. And even if I did, I was not about to disturb the slumber of my sweet roommate. She had been the first person—angel or human—to treat me as if I was worthy, so why would I repay her with fear? I couldn't say that to him though.

"Of course, Master. I have not left her side for more than a few minutes at a time," I lied. "If she has a secret, I will find it." I was not so sure I would, but why provoke his wrath? I was hoping he didn't have his other minions watching me.

"You better not be lying to me, angel." Then he cackled unexpectedly. "Like you would. You don't have half a brain and definitely not the balls to do that. Keep at it, minion. I'll check in with you again soon."

As much as it pained me to admit it, he was right; I was a spineless angel who lived in abject fear of what Asmodeus and the other higher angels would do to me if I didn't obey them. Even though hurting angels—light or dark—was against all angelic directives, the high angels of dark had no problem breaking the rules anytime they felt like it. And they felt like it often.

"Are you okay?" It was Joan, her hand on my forearm, brows furrowed over her intense honey-brown eyes.

I didn't deserve her concern. I was here to spy on her and, who knew, maybe even contribute to her demise, and yet she treated me as someone worthy of worry, worthy of attention and support. At that moment something shifted inside of me. Not that I had ever loved myself, but right then and there, I felt the toxic fumes of hate beginning to gather inside and toward me. I was a despicable creature.

## JOAN

I had tried everything I could think of. I bribed him with cookies, with coffee, even included an offer for whatever he wished. Nothing worked. Phoenix wouldn't snap out of the funk he'd been in since we visited my island. Did something there trigger bad memories for him? He wouldn't talk. In fact, he'd barely said a word since our short trip a couple days back. It was as if he had lost the power—or maybe the will—to speak, answering only with nods and low grunts.

It shouldn't have bothered me, but it did. We had only known each other for a couple months, but I couldn't deny I was more than a little attracted to him—physically and otherwise. Besides being outrageously gorgeous, Phoenix was humble, simple in tastes and needs, and always willing to help out. He was not shy but very reserved. When he smiled, it was as if the sun had landed in the room—not that he smiled much, but before the island trip, I had begun seeing that sexy, heart-melting smile more often. I wondered what he was hiding, because it was obvious he had a secret. He was awkward, surprised by the most common of things, almost like a child learning about the world around him for the first time. It pulled on my heartstrings and made me want to know him better.

"Come on, Nix. My brother is coming soon, and I have a whole plate full of snickerdoodle cookies waiting for you." I was outside his door, knocking and begging. Maybe if I was super annoying, he would capitulate and open the door. "Open the fucking door, Nix."

Footsteps preceded the telltale clicking of the lock on the door. I took a step back, waiting for it to open. His face, a perfect exercise in symmetry and sexy aesthetics, appeared from behind the door. "I'm all right, Joan. Just want to be alone for a while." It was like a mantra that he repeated every time I asked him for an explanation for his sudden change in mood.

"Bullshit. There is something wrong. I can tell." I held his hand and pulled him toward me. "Come and sit with me for a while. Let's talk."

He followed me silently, eyes on the ground. We sat on the couch, side by side, my legs curled under me. I studied him for a moment. There was such a dark sadness in his eyes that they seemed to have gone from hazel to black. I had asked Caleb to come over and try to figure out what was going on with Phoenix. Caleb had always been the wise one in our family duet, both a brother and a father since our parents had died in an accident. He was the one I always ran to for help, he and his fiancé, Sky, who I loved as family and who had lost his angel wings to protect my brother.

"Tell me what's wrong, Nix," I asked, leaning over to touch his hand. He flinched but didn't pull away. "Something happened at the island, and I want to know what it is. We're roommates, and I care for you." Maybe a little too much, considering that after a couple months of living together, I still felt like I barely knew him. The man was a mystery.

Phoenix did look at me then, his eyes still dark and wet. "I'm not who you think I am, and I can't tell you what I am." The confusion I was feeling must have shown on my face, because he added, "I don't have many memories of who I was or where I came from before becoming an adult. Being on the island, surrounded by that beauty, somehow struck me as a reminder of what I've been missing my whole life, that's all. I have done nothing worthy or useful, and I most definitely have never done anything beautiful. A waste of a life."

Without thinking, I sprang forward and wrapped my arms around him, pulling him close to me. At first, he stiffened, and for a moment I thought I had done the wrong thing. But as I was getting ready to release him from the embrace, his arms went around me, his hands flattening against my back, and his face nestled in the crook of my neck. He was all hard muscle, but his skin was soft and warm under the tips of my fingers.

*What now? Do I hold him, or do I let go?*

"You must be wrong, Nix." Not knowing what else to say, I babbled on about his worth and beauty, but I wasn't even sure he heard me. His breathing had gone so quiet that if it wasn't for the sure grip on my back, I would have thought he'd fallen asleep. As I always did when I was nervous, I kept talking about everything and nothing in particular. He kept silent until I, having run out of words, stopped chatting away.

"You're warm." Not the best compliment I'd ever been given, but somehow it felt as if it was. I shivered under his hold and felt my legs turn to mush. *Oh, fuck. This is not good.* "Why do you shake?"

When I didn't answer right away, he let me go suddenly, his face a sickly shade of gray and lips turned into a frown. "Did I hurt you? That's what I do; I hurt people. Even when I don't want to, I still do harm."

"No, that's not it at all," I exclaimed, grabbing his hand. I didn't want him to move away from me. It felt right having my body against his. "You didn't hurt me, I promise."

He blinked his eyes. "But you were shaking. You were scared of me."

"Oh my God, no." How could he think that? And what could I tell him to convince him otherwise? "Listen, Nix, I was shaking because it felt good in your arms. I was not scared. I was—" Shit. I was about to tell this guy I had the hots for him.

I didn't have to explain further though. His lips stretched into the warmest, sunniest smile I had seen in a while. "Really? You weren't even a little scared?"

Phoenix could be so puzzling sometimes. "Why would I be scared of you? Do you think I'd let you live in the room next to mine if I thought you were dangerous?"

He opened his mouth to answer, but a loud knock interrupted him. We both looked at the door at the same time, wondering who was interrupting our moment.

"Open up, sis. There's a breeze out here." It was Caleb's voice, the one that had always given me the comfort I needed in bad moments. My brother, my rock, and the biggest pain in my butt at times.

I got up to open the door and was immediately drawn into a bear hug. "Fuck, Caleb. You're strangling me."

Caleb let me go and scowled. "Still the same potty mouth, I see. If you're going to be a businesswoman, you better clean it, girl." He noticed my roommate for the first time. "Phoenix, I presume." My brother and his fiancé had been over a couple of times to help with the store, but they had never met Phoenix. Busy with their wedding preparations, Caleb and Sky had come straight to the café while I was at work and my roommate at home.

"Yes, this is my roommate." I moved between the two as Phoenix stood up. He was about as tall as my brother, and I looked like an ant in comparison. "This is my brother, Caleb."

Caleb shook his hand, and we all sat at the kitchen table, drinking coffee and eating cookies. Caleb and Phoenix talked while I watched them both. Caleb looked so much happier now than he had before he met Sky, another reason I loved my brother's angel.

Phoenix still didn't talk much, but he listened with interest and nodded at my brother's chatter. For once, I didn't talk. I liked watching my handsome and rather haunted roommate. There were so many questions I'd like to ask him but was afraid to, so many things I wanted to know about him, but one stood out at that moment: What were those two hard ridges I had felt when my fingers roamed his back?

✝

## NIX

My heart was still beating too fast. As an angel, my heart rate was normally pretty slow; it could even stop beating for a while without harming me. That hug had done something strange to my body and possibly my brain. In addition to my rapid heartbeat, my skin was tingly and warmer than usual, and an odd yearning for something I couldn't quite identify was gnawing at my gut. Not a feeling I could name, even though in the back of my mind it felt familiar.

I watched Joan as she exchanged snarky remarks with her brother, a tall, dark-haired man with the most unusual eyes I had ever seen, one green, the other lavender. Their conversation was a well-choreographed dance of give-and-take—obviously something they did often. Caleb repeatedly remarked on Joan's unwise choice of words, but she didn't listen and, in fact, seemed to make an extra effort at using all the language that bothered her brother. Something told me this struggle between them wasn't anything new.

"Well, shit, Caleb. Why didn't you bring your hot man with you?" Joan returned to the table with a fresh pot of coffee, closely followed by Caleb, munching distractedly on a cookie.

"He had a meeting with Gabriel." Caleb stole a furtive glance at me. "They needed to try the new—" He paused, coughed, and looked at me again from the corner of his eye. "You know, the new suit for the wedding."

Joan looked as if she was having fun, her full lips extended into a mischievous smile. "I'm surprised Gabriel didn't want some of my cookies," she said and winked. I couldn't follow their conversation at all and was baffled by the strange looks and smiles. "Caleb and his fiancé are getting married soon." It took me a moment to realize she was talking to me. "You're invited, of course."

Not sure what to say, I tried to smile and failed miserably. Smiling still didn't come naturally to me except when I smiled at my roommate. With her, everything was easy and natural, and I had to wonder if it didn't have something to do with the fact that she had been able to see me as an angel.

"You'll have to bring Sky to meet Phoenix. Nix sometimes reminds me of him." They exchanged another knowing look. "Maybe we could all go out one night."

Caleb groaned. "You know Sky and I don't do the club scene."

"You are both so old for your age," Joan said, crossing her arms over her chest like a little girl pouting. "One night in town won't kill you, and I think it will do Nix a whole lot of good. He's been a little blue lately."

Even though I couldn't totally understand what was happening between the two, I was enjoying it. I figured this was what humans called entertainment. Joan had introduced me to some TV shows, but we spent most of our evenings sitting on the couch either reading or talking quietly. For someone who didn't have many memories or much I could actually tell Joan, I enjoyed speaking with her. We talked about things we had done or seen that day, and she would tell me about the orange-haired man who worked for one of the local fisheries and thought of himself as God's gift to women. Her stories about the wacky people who worked with her or somehow crossed her path every day were interesting and amusing, and I waited anxiously all day to hear them. On Fridays, she had the day off, so we always ended up at her bakery, finishing up one thing or another and meeting with Tess at an eatery in the harbor.

It hadn't taken me long to come to the stunning conclusion that Joan fascinated me in ways I couldn't explain. I craved her presence and felt hollowed when she wasn't around. The thought that Asmodeus could harm her if she turned out to be a threat was unbearable, and I had been spending night after night trying to come up with a plan. I was crushed by the knowledge that I was powerless when facing my master. I was powerless no matter what. I was nothing but a minion, a servant who was allowed to live for one reason only: because Asmodeus could not be bothered doing the lesser tasks. I was only valuable as far as my master thought I was. I lived with the certainty that the day would come when Asmodeus wouldn't find any further use for me and would then end my life—what stood for death among the angels: eternal pain, clipped wings, isolation. Angels were not allowed to hurt other angels, but my master was an expert at breaking rules and getting away with it. The seraphic world had once been rocked by a case of an angel of light who had been captured and tortured by Asmodeus's minions before being rescued by one of the archangels. New angelic directives had been put in place to prevent that from happening again, but what Asmodeus wanted, he got. It didn't matter who was hurt in the process.

Caleb threw his hands over his head in surrender. "Okay, where do you want to go? We have to come over to check on the caterers, so we could stay later and go somewhere."

Joan's eyes brightened. "There's this new club I've been wanting to check out, the Dancing Lobster." Caleb burst out laughing and she giggled. "I kid you not, that's the name." That made her brother laugh even harder, and soon Joan joined him. Their laughter was so contagious, I found myself chuckling along with them, the fact that I had no idea what was so funny notwithstanding.

I had to admit that by the time Caleb stood to leave, I had almost forgotten my conversation with Asmodeus—or at least put it in some corner of my fuzzy memory so I could continue to enjoy my time with Joan here on Earth. We both followed Caleb to the door to say our goodbyes and stood in the doorway waving as her brother got into an Uber—could I ask her what that was without sounding like an idiot?—and drove away.

Joan turned around before I did, and the next thing I knew, she was in my arms again, her breasts crushed against me and her arms flying to anchor themselves on my arms. My hands went automatically to her waist, and I held her steady so she wouldn't fall. At first, I didn't think much of it until her eyes met mine. A fire erupted inside of me as I trailed my gaze to her cute nose and then to her lips. Her tongue flickered over her lips, and I had this sudden and weird urge to bend down and kiss her. Even stranger, she was rising on her tiptoes to meet me halfway. We were so close, I could feel her breath caress the sensitive skin of my lips, and the crack inside of me expanded and ran through my body and my soul. I couldn't understand it. This kind of desire was not familiar to me. As a lackey to the dark master, I was often used to appease some of Asmodeus's appetites, and the last thing I wanted was to feel what I always felt when my master took me down to his chamber of torture. Only this time, my legs didn't tremble in fear and my body didn't hurt in anticipation of what was to come. This time, I wanted it to happen. I wanted her lips on mine, her hands on my body. I wanted to—

"No, no." I pulled away from her, confused. I couldn't give in to the urge. Not that I was afraid of hurting her—I knew I wouldn't—but I was not worthy of her. My body and soul were soiled by evil. "Sorry."

I turned around and fled to hide in my room. I would not stain the one thing that was good in my miserable life.

# CHAPTER 5
## FALLING

## JOAN

This was getting ridiculous. No matter what I was doing, where I was, my thoughts kept drifting to my hot roommate. It was as if I were a tiny iron shaving with no hope of resisting the mighty pull of his magnetic field. It was becoming embarrassing—not to mention uncomfortable—that my face turned the color of a boiled lobster every time he came close to me. Or when he caught my eyes. Or when he sat in his lounging pants, all relaxed and sexy, while he devoured a book or two. His love for reading had raised his sexiness level to the top of the scale. Me, the wild one, had always been attracted to men with a taste for good fiction. There was something inherently hot about a man with a book.

Phoenix was still the same quiet man, only talking when spoken to, never making requests or demands. He kept his room immaculate, not a dust bunny in sight, effectively guilting me into being a bit more industrious when it came to cleaning the house. I had taught him to do the laundry, and he always smelled of fresh clothing and dryer sheets. I knew this because I shamelessly stole a sniff when he walked by.

He didn't sleep much. I heard him pacing in the room in the middle of the night, as if something in his mind wouldn't let him catch a snooze. Maybe his conscience. I was reminded of the conversation we'd had, and how he claimed he was not who I thought he was. I didn't know who he was, other than what I had seen and heard since he had come to live under my roof a couple of months ago. He seemed honorable enough, and he was always willing to offer a helping hand. Phoenix was more than happy to come to the bakery every Friday and sometimes after I came home from work to help me with fixing and decorating. He carried heavy items as if they weighed less than a feather duster and had a special gift to see things I couldn't—like the giant spider hiding in the corner underneath the sink.

"Where shall I put this?" I burst out laughing when he came in the room, holding up a cake mixer and wearing a silly frilly apron he must have dug out of one of my Halloween boxes. "What? What's so funny?"

"The apron." I snorted, covering my mouth with my hand. "You look so silly wearing that thing. That was from a costume party last Halloween."

Phoenix looked down at the apron and then back at me, two

quizzical eyebrows arched above his olive-green eyes. "I didn't want to get my pants dirty. The other pair is still in the washer." I was still laughing, trying not to spit out my gum. I really should take him shopping again. "I can take it off."

"No, you're fine. You just caught me by surprise." I moved toward him, still staring at the goofy garment. "I'm glad you're confident enough in your manhood to wear that."

"My manhood? What do you mean?" He always looked so confused. I had to wonder what kind of rural area he came from. "Do males like to get dirty?"

Sometimes it was not worth explaining things to him, and to be honest, I was not always sure he was serious. "Take that off and let's go get something to eat. I'm in the mood for a lobster roll."

A few minutes later, we were walking down toward the harbor where the cheapest lobster roll eateries were located. With it being early spring, dark had already descended upon us, cooling everything enough that the breeze made me shiver as we negotiated a corner of the street a block away from the bakery.

"Shit, it's getting cold." I rubbed my arms, desperate for whatever warmth I could produce from the friction. "When is spring actually going to get here?" Winter had been a long one, and even though it hadn't snowed in over a month, the air stuck stubbornly to winter-like temperatures.

Surprising me, Phoenix draped an arm over my shoulders and pulled me against his side. "Here, I'll warm you up." It was said in innocence, I was sure of it. Phoenix didn't seem to have one malicious bone in his body, but whatever he meant, he was sure successful at bringing heat into my skin—a bit too much. That slow-burning fire inside of me erupted to a full blaze as soon as he touched me.

*Damn, girl. Get it together.*

I hadn't dated in a while. After another painful experience with romance in my early days in college, I had decided to prioritize my future at the price of my social life, and his touch reminded me all too painfully of how long it had been since I dated anyone. For a moment I considered pushing him away, but it felt so wonderful that I couldn't make myself do it.

"Better?" he asked, rubbing my shoulder with his hand.

I decided not to lie. "Warmer, that's for sure." I coughed, embarrassed by my reaction to him. "Thank you. I should have brought a coat." He didn't have one either, yet his body was as warm as a fleece blanket.

"We're partners, right?"

Work partners maybe, but I was pretty sure they weren't supposed to feel like I did toward him.

I was quiet for the rest of the way. Phoenix let go of me when we walked in the small restaurant, and I felt stupidly bereft. We sat in one of the small wooden booths and ordered two lobster rolls and a couple of hot cocoas. "Lobster and chocolate." I giggled, still slightly inebriated from his touch. "Boy, there's a combination right there."

"Not a good one?" He slid onto the seat beside me instead of the one facing me, and our bodies were once again touching a bit too intimately for comfort—or at least it felt that way.

I shifted in my seat, restless. "Probably not, but no risk no gain, right?"

"Right." He went quiet and stared beyond me at the harbor water, glittering under the light of the moon. I was so intent on how I felt having my hip against his, my shoulder touching his arm, that I almost jumped out of my skin when his hand covered mine. He looked at me with a question in his eyes. "Is this okay?" he said.

I hoped my eyes spoke loud and clear. This was better than okay. This was amazing.

## NIX

Nerves were taking over my whole being. I didn't remember ever being nervous. Scared, yes. Terrified, many times, but nervous? I didn't think so. Despite all that, I was indeed a nervous wreck as Joan dressed in her room next to mine. We had been spending a lot of time together, not just keeping each other company or sharing the work at the bakery but also getting closer. That day at the harbor restaurant while waiting for our lobster rolls, I had lost all common sense and held her hand. It was a simple gesture, but, considering my mission on Earth, it was also extremely reckless. How stupid was I to be having these strange, warm feelings toward the one woman I was to keep an eye on? The same mortal my master couldn't wait to see "taken care of." I thanked the heavens above that time moved slower at the Fortress and that Asmodeus didn't seem to have noticed how much time had already passed since he had sent me on this mission.

Her brother and his fiancé would be meeting us at this—what was the name she called it?—nightclub for a night on the town. Joan was full of these quirky expressions that meant little to me, but her voice sounded like music to my ears. I couldn't be sure what that entailed, but being out with her and also under the scrutiny of her brother was having a strange effect on me.

"Are you ready, Cinderella?" Joan yelled out from behind my door. I had been sitting on the edge of my bed, staring at the wall with a knot in my throat and sweat collecting in the palms of my hands. For once I was wishing for the comfortable, however sparse angelic clothing, as the jeans and T-shirt I was wearing squeezed and rubbed against my skin. But there was no more avoiding the inevitable.

"Coming," I yelled back, forcing my numb legs to support my weight. What was going on with me?

Joan was waiting, a vision in a pair of skinny black jeans and a skintight black tank top cinched at the waist by a double belt with a golden buckle. Black high-heeled ankle boots and a white jacket completed the outfit that left me breathless. Much to Joan's fashion, she wore no jewelry or any other frills, her hair simply combed loose around her oval face, and I coughed out an inaudible "you look beautiful" before choking on my own tongue.

"Are you sick or something?" She braced her hands on her hips and tapped her foot impatiently. "Caleb is already at the club. I called an Uber."

Like a sheep, I followed her out, trying hard not to trip over my feet every time I caught sight of her perfectly shaped bottom, emphasized by the tight pants. "What exactly is a nightclub?" I finally managed to ask.

She whipped her head around and stared at me as if I had lost my mind. "You're kidding me, right?" No, I absolutely was not. "A club where people go to listen to music and dance. There might be some drinking involved."

Music? Dancing? Drinking? I was in trouble. Even though human myths had angels flying around with harps in their hands, dark angels didn't listen to music ever. I had never danced, and drinking was the root of all evil—or so I'd heard. What was I doing?

I didn't have much time to dwell on it. As soon as the so-called Uber arrived, Joan practically shoved me in the back seat and slid in beside me. "The Dancing Lobster, please." The driver nodded and took off even before the door was completely closed.

Cars were not a mystery to me. I had plucked more than one soul from vehicles crushed into a mangled pile of metal, but I had never driven in one. It was both exhilarating and terrifying. Flying was not the same—when I flew, I was in control of the turns and twists. In this car I had no control as the vehicle whipped this way and that, throwing me into Joan or against the door as if we were in zero gravity.

Joan laughed under her breath. "What's so funny?" I was sure my voice betrayed the fear gripping my senses and nerves.

"You look like someone is chasing you with a shotgun." A gurgling of laughter escaped her lips, and she covered her mouth to muffle it.

Perplexed, I stared at her. "You're not scared we're going to end up crushed under this car?"

Something I said had a surprising effect on her. Her smile vanished and was replaced by a quivering lip as she was on the verge of tears. Damn it. What had I done now?

Hesitantly, I held her hand. "What did I say? Why are you upset?"

She shook her head but didn't say anything at first. Patience was my only virtue, so I waited. "My parents died in a car accident," she finally said, so softly I almost didn't hear it. "Both my brother and I were in the car with them when it happened."

Fuck! I knew that—at least the part about her parents dying in an accident—so what had possessed me to say something like that? Fear, I guess. Fear had always been the one thing that blinded me to all else, the one emotion that drove my days and my nights. I had no recollection of anything else. I was a coward, a worthless creature, a nothing. I had allowed fear to control me again, to cause me to be insensitive to the one person I wished to please, not harm.

"I'm sorry, Joan. I'm an idiot." What else could I say?

Joan squeezed my hand. "No, you're not. How could you have known?" Was she really forgiving me? "It's been a long time, but once in a while it still hits me out of nowhere—this terrible memory of my parents dying right next to me and the hopelessness I felt then."

I licked my lips and squeezed her hand back. "I'm sorry you

lost them."

"Me too, but they went to a good place." What did she mean by that? Hadn't she told me they were dead? "An angel of light collected their souls."

My body froze. Did she mean that literally, or was it another one of her quirky expressions? "An angel?"

She pulled her hand away and shook her head with a giggle. "A story for another day," she said, stealing a glance out the window. "We're here." Before I could ask her any more questions, the car stopped with a loud screech, and Joan opened the door and jumped out. "Come on. I see Sky."

I was paralyzed for a moment. Coming from anyone else, I would have ignored her comment, but this was the same woman who had seen me when I was plucking a soul. Was it possible that she could see all angels? And how did she know which ones were angels of light or of dark? What secret was this amazing creature hiding, and would it be her demise?

After a while I followed her out of the car. She finished paying the driver, and not waiting any longer, she looped her arm through mine and tugged me along toward the building. Music reached my ears as I took in the scene around us. Outside the building, a small throng of people loitered under the streetlights, some smoking, some talking, a couple engaged in a kiss. A blond, tall man waved at us and called to Joan.

"That's my brother's boyfriend," Joan said. "Hey, Sky. This is my roommate, Nix."

"Hello, Nix. Pleasure to meet you. Any friend of Joan is a friend of mine." A surge of recognition sparked as our hands touched. I had never seen him, I was sure of that, but he somehow felt familiar. I thought he gave me a look, but I probably imagined it because one minute it was there, the next it was gone. "Caleb is inside getting us a table."

All my doubts and worries were wiped the moment I entered the club. The large room inside was dipped in semidarkness where all the stars in the sky had come to settle, moving colorful lights that flickered over everything and everyone. The sound assailed my ears with such violence, I had to cover them. There was nothing peaceful or melodic about what Joan was calling music, merely a collection of loud, unconnected noises that scratched at my eardrums like claws.

Joan laughed. "It takes a while to get used to," she said. I wasn't so sure. "Let's dance."

Before we even reached the table where her brother waited for us, my human grabbed my hand and dragged me to the center of the room where several people moved to the screeching noise, obviously enjoying themselves. I was about to protest when the music changed into a soft, slow melody that caressed all my senses and lulled me into a feeling of serenity. I was not expecting it, and I almost jumped out of my skin when Joan slid her hands over my shoulders and pulled me closer until our bodies were glued together. Dark angels would never be admitted into Arcadia, but right then I had arrived at my own private heaven.

# JOAN

In hindsight, it wasn't the smartest thing I'd ever done. But Jesus, it was toe-curling amazing. Having his hard body crushed against mine as we slowly swayed to the music was heavenly. If I wasn't so focused on how my body had been seized by waves of heat and electricity, I would have laughed. I had to lead because Mr. Hotness had no idea what to do once we were in each other's arms.

I flattened my cheek against his chest, discovering—much to my pleasure—his heart beating as if a drum line had taken up residence there. He wasn't totally unaffected by me after all, no matter how aloof he always appeared. Encouraged by his reaction, I swept a hand over the small of his back slowly and, I hoped, meaningfully. I felt him stiffen, and I cursed my tendency to be too forward. Guys hated that. But then his muscles relaxed under my hand and yielded against me. My body followed suit, each muscle relaxing just as a fire ignited in my gut.

What the hell was I doing? I had sworn off men after my last romantic entanglement in college. Men were pigs with no hearts. That had been my mantra for the past year or so. Why was I giving in now? Granted, despite the weird feeling that I'd met him before, Phoenix was different from all the guys I had ever met. After my brother met Sky, I had done nothing but dream of finding that kind of love, that kind of relationship. I had no such luck. My latest boyfriend—one in a string of disastrous relationships I'd had since my teens—had sworn his eternal love for me only to run for the hills when a false-positive pregnancy test came between us. All men were untrustworthy unless they were Caleb or Sky, which left me with the tiniest hope of ever finding my soul mate.

"Is it always like this?" Phoenix leaned over to whisper in my ear. His warm breath made all the muscles in my body clench in pleasure.

"What is?" I managed to squeak out, my face still squashed onto his chest and unwilling to move. It felt too good there.

His rich voice vibrated against my ear. "Dancing. Is it always this—" He paused for a moment. "—wonderful?"

I did lift my face to him then, what I was certain was a big, goofy smile splashed across my lips. "No, not always."

His eyes danced in their sockets, the strobe lights making them twinkle like stars. Phoenix did what he rarely did; he smiled. When Phoenix smiled, the sun emerged from nowhere and graced us with its warmth and light. I rose on my tiptoes, foregoing any control, and our faces moved closer in a collision course for a kiss. My eyes looked to his luscious lips and a flutter of butterflies swarmed inside me, but as our lips were a breath apart, someone grabbed my shoulder and pulled me away.

"Caleb!" For the first time in a long while, I entertained murderous thoughts about my brother. "What the fuck?"

Caleb rolled his eyes, his usual reaction to my cussing, and gestured toward a table where Sky was sitting, sipping a colorful drink and waving at us. "Let's sit for a bit," he said, raising his voice above the music and leading us away from the dance floor.

Now that our bodies were apart, I felt as if something was missing. It was mystifying to me that the mere proximity of someone's body could cause such a reaction, but now I wanted to explore the sensation and take it to another level altogether. My brother was effectively dampening the whole experience.

"We got you drinks," Sky said as soon as we sat at the table. "Phoenix, I don't know what you drink, so I ordered the same thing as Joan. She's a slosh." I gave him the stink-eye and he laughed.

Phoenix looked at the large cup and then at me, his eyebrows lifted. "It's a margarita," I told him with a shrug. "Tequila, orange liqueur, and lime juice. It's very good." I was not sure he should drink it though. I had never heard him talk about alcoholic drinks, and judging from what I knew about him, I would wager he had never had one.

Hesitantly, he brought the salted rim to his lips, and I involuntarily licked my lips, imagining tasting the tang of the salt and the sweetness of his lips on my tongue. He took a sip and grimaced, his mouth twisting into a comical frown. I laughed and he smiled at me before taking another sip. "Not sure I like it," he said, putting the cup down. "I love the heat of it going down my throat, but the taste… I don't know."

Desperate for something I couldn't have in my mouth, I gulped down a quarter of the cocktail, relishing the burn down my throat and the tartness left behind on my tongue. Phoenix stared at me, his eyes two large saucers, his lips slightly apart. Was he thinking the same as me? Suddenly I wanted to get out of there, grab a ride, and go home where I could be alone with my roommate and explore the scenarios my fertile imagination was flooding my mind with. Considering my brother and his fiancé had driven all the way to Boothbay Harbor to go clubbing with me, I had to give up on the idea of an escape and soldier on through an evening of torturous sexual tension.

"Come with me, will you?"

Sky's request took me by surprise. I threw a questioning look at my brother and then followed him outside, where the cold night air slapped me out of whatever trance I was in. I hugged myself since I'd left my jacket inside and my tank top was hardly a good choice of outfit for the crisp nocturnal temperature.

Sky, as usual, was not cold at all. At times like this I was really jealous of his angelic blood. "What's up, Sky? Did your wings come in finally?" Archangel Gabriel had been trying to get Sky new prosthetic wings so he could fly again. The first ones the angelic engineers magicked had not lasted long or worked well. I didn't know much about flying other than in an airplane, but Sky assured us that the gadget was heavy and cumbersome, not allowing for the magic and weightlessness feeling of flight at all. For the past year and a half, Gabriel had been working to come up with better ones. It was the least he could do after what Sky had gone through at the hands of Samael, one of Asmodeus's favorites.

"Yes, they did. They're amazing." Sky's blue eyes lit up. "Not the same as my wings, but close enough. I went on my first flight last Saturday, and it was awesome. I had almost forgotten how I loved flying."

I doubted that very much. Flying had been Sky's only love before meeting my brother. Losing his wings in such a cruel way had been a brutal blow.

"I'm happy for you, dude." I wrapped my hands around his neck and hugged him, my toes lifting off the ground and almost taking off.

"But that's not why I called you out here." I was all ears now. "Phoenix. What do you know about him?"

That was an odd question. "He's a nice, quiet guy who helps me out every chance he has and asks nothing in return." Shit. I really didn't know much about his life before me, did I? The weird thing was that he didn't either. "Why?"

Sky scratched his forehead. "I don't know. There is something about him…." He caught his lower lip between his teeth, his eyes focused on nothing in particular. "It may be nothing, but I felt something when I shook his hand—a recognition of sorts. Can't explain it. It was weird and unexpected, and I want you to be aware of it and be careful."

I guffawed. "You know me. Caution is my middle name."

"No, it's not. Your middle name is Marie." Even after all this time, Sky still had problems understanding sarcastic remarks. He had that in common with Phoenix, who seemed to be oblivious to jokes. "Just watch him closely, okay?"

I had all intentions of watching him from a close angle, hopefully one without much space at all between us. "I promise I'll keep that in mind," I said, a smile on my lips. I was always touched by Sky's concern about me. He had taken on the role of my protector very seriously, even though I could take care of myself just fine. "Don't you worry about me, silly angel. You worry about your impending nuptials. I'm so excited for the two of you." I gave him another hug.

We chatted about the wedding for a bit, effectively distracting him from Phoenix and me. After a while I felt as if the North Pole had settled inside me, so we went back inside and joined the others. I could tell by the smirk on Caleb's face that he had been grilling poor Phoenix who looked as panicked and confused as Daffy Duck.

"Has he been asking you a million questions?" I asked, leaning over to him.

Phoenix smiled hesitantly. "Yes. Is that normal?"

I chuckled. "For my brother? Yes, totally. He thinks he's my father."

My roommate looked even more confused. "But he's your brother, isn't he?"

Caleb and I burst out laughing. I laughed so hard, tears rolled down my cheeks. It was then, as I wiped the droplets from my eyes, that I saw it: Phoenix and Sky had the same exact expression on their faces. One was light, the other dark, but there was something eerily similar about them. How had I never noticed it before?

# NIX

I woke up in a sweat, my heart trotting in my chest. My nightmare was still vivid in my mind, terrifying images that stuck to my retinas and refused to be erased. I sat up in bed, mouth as dry and gritty as sand, and feeling a bit disoriented. Had I screamed, or had I imagined it?

"Nix, are you okay?" Joan's voice came through the wooden door muffled but clearly worried. I must have screamed after all. "Let me in."

I took a couple deep breaths, trying to slow down the beating of my heart and failing. I swung my legs over the side of the bed and stood up, noticing how wobbly my limbs were. It took me longer than it should have to get to the door and open it. Joan was standing there, gorgeous as ever in her printed pajamas and a worried frown. When my eyes met hers, a shiver of something I didn't recognize ran over me. I couldn't hold her gaze for long, so I stared at my feet.

"I heard you scream." I may have not been able to see it, but I could feel it—her eyes burrowed holes in my heart.

"I had a nightmare," I said, not daring to look up. "I'm fine. Go back to bed."

Joan was silent for a moment, and I risked a glance. She was closer than I thought, so close I could touch her without having to stretch my arm. I wasn't sure whether I really could feel her heat or if I was imagining it. She took another step closer, and I had a moment of insanity; I imagined taking her in my arms and kissing her. My mind reeled, confused by my recurring wish to kiss Joan; kissing was part of an unpleasant routine that I had no wish of participating in ever again. At the Fortress I stayed as invisible as I could, so Asmodeus would not call me to be part of one of his games.

"What's wrong? You've been acting weird off and on since the island trip," Joan said, taking yet another step forward. I instinctively matched her with a step backward. She flinched. "Sorry. I didn't mean to invade your personal space. I'll get out of your hair."

The hurt in her voice moved something inside of me. Before she could leave, I held on to her arms and pulled her to me. "No, please don't." It was a plea for mercy. I had never encountered the kind of care and companionship she was willing to offer me. "I don't want you out of my personal space."

Our eyes met and I drank her in, like a man who had lived in a desert all his life and was parched for what those eyes were promising. After a moment of hesitation, she inched over again and, standing on her tiptoes, locked her lips with mine. I was not expecting what came next; instead of the disgust and wish to flee that kisses always brought on, a wave of warmth and pleasure washed over my whole being. Her lips were soft and yielding, parted and inviting. I wasn't sure how I knew what to do, but I accepted her invitation and tasted the sweetness in her tongue. I rode the spiraling storm of sensations her lips had unleashed inside of me, in a mixture of awe and fear. I could get used to that, which wasn't a good thing, knowing I'd be back to the dark world that I called home, where I would never again be allowed to feel like this.

Joan's hands had found their way under my T-shirt, the tip of her fingers exploring the ridges and valleys of the muscles on my back, a thrilling caress, strangely familiar and unsettling. I moaned against the soft skin of her lips and felt myself swell against her. That was madness. Sex was not a pleasant thing, was not something I ever longed for, so why was I yearning for Joan's touch? Craving to feel her skin against my naked body?

"You feel so good," Joan whispered, her lips playing havoc with my senses as she peppered kisses along my chin, the side of my neck, my earlobe.

I wanted to tell her she felt good too, but my mouth refused to articulate the words. Instead, I mimicked her actions and began covering her face, neck, and shoulder with kisses. Blinded to everything else, my hands slipped under her pajama top, a bluish cotton T-shirt appropriately decorated with lipstick prints. When my fingers met the soft mounds of her breasts, I swelled further, a frantic but pleasant urgency building up within the flames in my gut.

"I want you too." Maybe Joan was a witch, or some other magical creature who could read minds, because I was sure I hadn't uttered those words stuck in my throat.

She tugged on my T-shirt and pulled it over my head, brushing her palms slowly down my chest, lingering for a while on my pecs. She looked up at me, her eyes shining with undisguised desire, and then replaced her hands with her lips, flicking her tongue across my overly sensitive skin. I moaned again.

"Are you going to undress me?" she asked, her fingers now playing with the string that held my sweats around my hips, tantalizingly close to my arousal.

She didn't have to ask twice. In no time I stripped her of her pajamas, and she stood before me gloriously bare except for her panties. Not wanting her to be the only one so exposed, I shrugged off my sweatpants. "Now we're equal," I said.

Joan giggled and scanned me from top to bottom, the heat in her eyes making me tingle all over as effectively as her hands. "You're beautiful, Nix," she whispered, her voice thick and hoarse. "You're so perfectly beautiful."

I opened my mouth to protest, but she had already glued her body to mine, her hand low between us, working on what I had thought impossible—making me swell further until I was sure I'd explode. This was new and wonderful, but why did it also feel familiar and sad? A memory tugged in the back of my mind, so hazy and blurred that I couldn't make much sense of it, but strong enough to give me pause. What was I remembering?

Our underwear had mysteriously joined the pile of discarded clothes on the floor of my room. Joan closed the door behind her with her foot, never stopping her surge of caresses, her hands expertly loosening groans and moans from me. She pushed me gently until the back of my legs hit the edge of the bed. "Lie down, Nix. I've been dreaming about this for a while now."

She had dreamed about us together like this?

I scooted backward onto the bed until my legs no longer

dangled from the edge, and she climbed on and kneeled next to me with a sigh. "Fuck, Nix. I'm so turned on, I may explode," she said.

Without giving me time to respond, she leaned over and began trailing her tongue from the base of my neck, over my chest, the hard muscles of my belly, and then lower still. I couldn't resist it and tilted my hips against her mouth. My life didn't allow many heavenly moments, but that was the word that kept creeping into my mind right then. Heavenly. Her touch was paradise. Her kiss was home.

✛

<h1 style="text-align:center">JOAN</h1>

I had the reputation of being a wild one. My high school friends, my neighbors, even my brother had always been convinced I was a free-spirited girl who slept with whomever she pleased, one tiny notch away from being labeled promiscuous. Granted, I had done nothing to contradict the myth; much to the contrary, I had often encouraged it. I'd realized early on that if everybody thought you were a savvy, worldly female, you were treated differently.

The truth was I was none of those things. My lifestyle, other than my potty mouth, was pretty tame. I was hardly a virgin, but some of my boyfriends with whom I had not had sex would never admit it unless tied to a lie detector; even though they complained about my reluctance to let them in my pants, they preferred the reputation to the contrary so the legend continued. Not that I was known as loose or a slut, but I was lauded as cool and forward thinking. If they only knew the truth.

Wanting Phoenix was making me into the woman people thought I was. With him I did feel wild and free, uninhibited and adventurous, the opposite of what I was in the romance zone. I licked him from his neck to areas of his body I had dreamed about but never thought I'd see, and he tasted better than dark chocolate melted into strong, high-quality coffee. When he moved his hips up to meet my lips, I shivered with anticipation but backed off for a moment. I wanted to look at him, to drink in the hard beauty he was, all lean muscle and smooth olive skin. He groaned in protest but allowed me to peruse his body. Tattooed across his chest, starting over the sternum and stretching in a crescendo, there was a flock of small black birds flying up and beyond his left shoulder. I stared at it, mesmerized.

"It's beautiful," I said, tracing the design with my fingers. Phoenix trembled beneath my touch. "Your tattoo, it's beautiful."

He looked at me as if he didn't know what I was talking about and covered my hand lying on his chest. "You're the one who's beautiful, Jo."

It was the first time he gave me a nickname, and for some reason that hit me as the sexiest thing he could have done. And the sweetest. I tore my eyes from the tattoo and focused on the rest of him, the glorious work of art of his body.

"I'm going to love you so hard, you'll beg for mercy." I was fully aware I was babbling, but I couldn't control myself. It was as if someone I didn't recognize had taken over my body and my libido.

I felt it before I could actually see it, the shift in his mood. His body stiffened beneath my hands, and his eyes filled with tears. Before I could do anything about it, he had sat up and slid his legs off the edge of the bed, back curved like an old man's and head between his hands. Confused, I sat next to him and placed my hand on his shoulder where the black birds disappeared and dipped back down across his shoulder blade. He flinched at my touch and my heart dropped. What had I done? The beautiful, vital man I had been caressing a few minutes earlier had shriveled into a broken creature.

"What happened? Did I say something wrong?" The last thing I wanted to do was hurt him in any way. My body was still on fire with longing, and I had to refrain from touching him since he didn't seem to want me anymore. Was he a male version of the stereotypical tease? *No, you fool. He's obviously hurting.* "Tell me, Nix, what's wrong? I want to help."

"I want to be alone, Joan." No more endearing nickname. I was back to being plain old Joan, the roommate. His eyes never rose from the floor. "Please."

I didn't want to leave. I wanted to wrap him in my arms and cover him in kisses until whatever was hurting him faded away. Shit. I was falling hard already. It would be pretty douchey of me to go against his wishes, so I stood and collected my discarded clothes while searching for words to comfort him—an impossible task, considering I didn't know what I should be comforting him for.

Even though I was as naked as he was, I was shocked by the fact that he seemed utterly vulnerable and fully aware of it. My stomach was tied in knots, twisted by the sorrow reflected in his posture.

"I'll go, Nix, but please don't shut me out," I pleaded, tears choking me. "I care for you, I really do, and I'm sorry if I caused you any pain. I thought you were as much into making love as I was, but I guess I was wrong. Come to me when you're ready to talk about it."

I left the room, closing the door quietly behind me and effectively setting up a wall between us. The carpet tickled the soles of my feet as I ran to my room and threw myself on top of my bed, tears burning in my eyes, begging to be released. It figured that the one time I opened up to a guy, I'd get rejected.

Was I rejected though? It was more as if Phoenix rejected himself, the man he'd been when we were entangled in bed, the man who'd surrendered to my touch with abandon.

I wiped the tears from my cheeks, blew my nose, and stretched on the cool bed coverings. My skin was still alive and too sensitive against the soft material beneath me, so I flopped onto my back, my right hand on my belly and my eyes on the ceiling. Years ago, right after Caleb had met his lovely fiancé, I had bought a stick-on mural, a cheap—but still beautiful—replica of a rather unknown painting of a fallen angel. I had always been fascinated by the way the artist had depicted the angel's despair so vividly; I could actually feel it every time I looked at it. I had picked that one in particular as a reminder of what sweet Sky had gone through to protect my brother and me, but just then, as I lay in bed gazing at it in the semidarkness, I saw something else altogether—somebody else.

The poster of the fallen angel in the painting was an exact replica of Phoenix's expression when I'd left his room.

I sat up, assailed by a sudden suspicion. Was it possible? Could Phoenix be a fallen angel? No, impossible. What were the odds of both me and my brother falling in love with angels? I shook my head and dismissed the preposterous idea with a sigh.

# CHAPTER 6
### REVELATION

## NIX

Did I sleep or just block the outside world from my thoughts, as I'd done so many times at the Fortress? I knew that at some point, I would need to get up and go on with life as it was, but I didn't have the strength to move yet. So I lay there, curled upon myself like a baby within the womb and just as naked, eyes open but not seeing. *Block it, block it.* My usual mantra. Sometimes it worked, other times not so much. I had learned long ago that I either figured a way to block certain events in my miserable, dark life or I would go insane—not that angels could go insane. Or could they?

After the bliss of Joan's hands on me, her words opened the gates to a flood of dark memories. None of them too recent, but bad memories seemed to take root deeper than any others. I'd been successful the past few years at being invisible to my master by following the rules: keep your eyes down, your back curved, don't make waves, don't let him notice you're around. Being noticed by Asmodeus was something I doubted any dark angel wished, but he had his favorites. I'd been one of them. His fixation with me had started deep into the fogs of my past, so far from recent memory that I couldn't identify the precise moment he had taken an unhealthy appetite for my body and soul—unhealthy for me, anyway. He seemed to fully enjoy it.

Every time he called me to his room of torture, I told myself I deserved it. I must have. Whatever I did to become a dark angel must have been far worse than the others' sins, because I was one of the few who had membership to Asmodeus's club of horrors. When he was done with me, I was sent to my quarters, broken into smaller pieces, both physically and spiritually. My angel body healed quickly, but my soul did not.

Joan had taken me briefly to what I imagined was heaven. Our connection had gone further than the physical. I felt something I couldn't even remember clearly, something I thought was happiness. The way she touched me, the things she whispered to me, had made me feel worthy, whole. Joan had me believe I was not dirtier than dirt, darker than sin. She told me I was beautiful and coaxed me into a state of wonderment and ecstasy with her lips and her fingers. Nothing close to that had ever come out of one of the many encounters with Asmodeus, in what he called the room of pleasure but we, the unfortunate few, called the torture room. My dark master was not above treating a few of his angels the same way he treated the darkest of souls condemned to an eternity of pain. The word mercy was ironically—because nothing Asmodeus did in that room had anything to do with mercy—one of his favorites during his "pleasure sessions." He often ordered me to beg for mercy, which I did and I'd meant every time, unleashing a wave of self-hate; I should have been stronger and stood up to him, I should have fought… but he was the one with all the angelic power. I had nothing I could use against him.

The familiar self-loathing made me twitch and I curled even further, my head now touching my knees. What had I done? Joan sounded hurt and confused when she left me to my misery. She had offered to help, to comfort me afterward, but those words—beg for mercy—held a power stronger than me. Asmodeus had left me alone for a long time now, but the fear he could notice me again was fresh in my mind. This thing with Joan placed me in the spotlight again, the one place I did not want to be.

Not her fault.

No, absolutely not her fault. For the first time, someone was treating me as if I were a valuable member of creation and not a spineless sinner who deserved to be punished over and over again, and I'd shunned her. What if she would not forgive me? Not that I deserved it, but she had seen light in me and given me hope—hope that maybe, just maybe, I had a chance at happiness.

With a groan, I unraveled from the ball I had wrapped myself into and picked up my clothes from the floor. As I moved around the room, I caught a glimpse of myself reflected in the mirror. I stopped and stared. That mirror image was me, a body that until the night before had known nothing but pain. I tried to see it like Joan saw it. Beautiful? Maybe. There was beauty in darkness. I couldn't see past it, but Joan somehow could. She looked through the soot of my soul and glimpsed light. Did that mean I had light inside of me? Was there a chance of salvation for me?

The tiny seed of hope had taken root, and I couldn't decide whether that was a good or bad thing.

⸸

## JOAN

I was hoping the warm smell of chocolate chip cookies—turned out they were his favorite—would pull Phoenix out of hiding. He'd been in his room for almost three days, and other than the sound of footsteps, I couldn't tell whether he was alive or dead. I assumed he was alive since the food and platters of cookies I'd been placing outside the door before I went to work in the morning were gone by the time I came back. He also must have been venturing out of the room when I was at work, because the dishes were always washed and dried, the floor swept, and anything I had left out of place was returned to its proper spot. It was not ideal, but it was at least encouraging.

I fanned the delicious scent toward his room with a kitchen towel and then went to the front door. I opened it, closed it, and then waited patiently without moving as much as a finger. Phoenix had the ears of a freaking cat and could detect sounds nobody else could. After a while I began cursing myself for the lack of insight to have placed a stool by the door so I could sit down while I waited and maybe read a book or something. My legs were going numb, and my mind, not used to doing nothing, was going batshit crazy. Soon I would have to move and forfeit the deception.

Just as I was about to give up, the door to his room cracked open and slowly swung in. I couldn't see inside the room from where I stood, and I held my breath, afraid to spook him away. Phoenix stepped into view, wearing a pair of old joggers we had bought at a secondhand store and no shirt. My gut and other parts of my body clenched. A wave of heat swept through me, leaving me breathless. All of a sudden, I imagined kneeling beside him on the bed, running my fingers over his naked body, all the feelings surging back to me.

He followed the smell into the kitchen, slumping over with a frown on his face. I watched him for a moment, not betraying my presence yet. I loved the way the soft pants hung low on his hips, revealing the lovely abs and the sexy V of his pelvic bones. A part of me liquefied.

Before I could control it, I let out a loud sigh, and he turned around. He squinted, his brow knitted into a bunch of tiny wrinkles. All I wanted to do was run into his arms and let him comfort me, calm this ache inside me, sate my hunger for him. I stood still instead, waiting.

"You didn't go to work," he said. When I shrugged, he asked,

"Why didn't you?"

Aware I had to tread carefully, I didn't move. "I wanted to talk to you, to find out if you were okay."

He stared at his bare feet. "I'm fine. You can go." As if I would, knowing I had done or said something that triggered his sudden withdrawal. "You should go."

Not sure if it was his insistence or this overwhelming need to be near him, but I threw caution to the wind and charged in his direction. He flinched but didn't move when I placed my hands on his arms. "I'm not going, Phoenix. You have to tell me what happened." Tears pushed against my resolve. "I can't stand that I hurt you and I don't even know why or how."

"Memories… bad memories," he whispered as if that would explain everything. "Something you said brought them back."

"Whatever it was, I didn't mean it, Nix. All I wanted was to—" I stumbled. What if I said the wrong thing again? "All I wanted was to make love to you, that's all."

Phoenix tilted his head in a birdlike way. "Make love? Was that what we were doing?" It was scary how young he sometimes sounded, but he couldn't be younger than me. He looked about the same age as my brother or Sky. Of course, Sky was a lot older than he looked, being an angel and all.

"Yes, of course. What did you think we were about to do?" Despite everything, I was now curious.

"Sex." Okay, so he wasn't totally innocent after all.

"It's the same, Nix. Po-tay-to, po-tah-to." He looked at me

as if I had grown an extra head. "Sex and making love are kind of the same. The only difference is one is only physical, and the other involves—" Shit, I'd been about to say love. *Too soon, Joan. Too fucking soon.* "It involves emotions, feelings."

"No pain?"

What the hell was he talking about? Why would making love bring on pain? "No, of course not. What makes you think there would be pain involved?" Bewildered, I zoomed in on his eyes, trying to get a better read on his thoughts. "I'm not into that kind of thing, Nix."

His eyes softened and his back straightened, a smile spreading across his lips. "No? I was afraid we'd hurt each other in the end."

I was still mystified. "Did I hurt you?"

Suddenly the heat was there again, in his eyes, in his smile, in his touch. "No, it was wonderful. I just thought—" he said with a sigh. "I have a complicated life."

You could say that again. Even though I couldn't figure out why he would think something so outrageous, I didn't think I should pursue it any longer. Maybe at a different time, he'd be willing to discuss it a bit more clearly. The last thing I wanted to do then was bring that cloud over him.

"Next time, ask me," I told him, gently squeezing his arm. "Okay?"

"Will there be a next time?"

Furious heat rose to my cheeks. Damn. He could throw me off balance with only a few words. I hoped there would be a next time. Soon. I was still tingling from his touch, and sleep had not come easy the past couple nights.

"You better believe it." I couldn't be sure I spoke those words aloud. I rose on my tiptoes and kissed him. "Unfortunately, I have to go to work now. Come pick me up this afternoon, please. Do you remember how to get to the lab?"

He nodded, a silent promise that left me almost giddy with happiness. Before I could walk away, he bent down and melded his warm lips with mine, deeper and longer than I had. I sighed into his mouth and made myself pull away. I couldn't be late, no matter what my heart and my body wanted. Until my bakery was open and making a profit, I needed that job.

I pulled away and ran to the door, afraid I wouldn't leave if I so much as glanced his way. Before I closed the door behind me, I thought I heard him say, "I love you," but I was sure I'd imagined it.

Could it be? Could I be in love with him?

## NIX

The words making love kept echoing in my mind. I couldn't be sure, but they sounded wondrous. A pleasant warmth ran through my body and settled in my heart every time I thought about it. Love. I'd heard about it, mostly when plucking souls from Earth in overheard conversations between mortals. I hadn't paid much attention to it then, but the words had always stayed with me, resonating as something oddly familiar. Something from my forgotten past, maybe. When Joan left for work, I couldn't control myself and the words escaped me. I told her I loved her, even though I didn't know what love really was or felt like. Fragments of lost memories kept flashing in my head: words whispered under the sheets, a touch, a kiss, a hesitant profession of love in the darkness of night. What was I remembering? As far as I knew, I'd always been Asmodeus's lowly servant, there to do his bidding, to suffer at the hands of his wicked self, tortured, violated, humiliated. A reluctant creature of darkness.

I couldn't remember what I did all day. Probably nothing. I was still inside my head when a knock from the door snapped me into reality. Who could it be? In all the time I'd lived with Joan, the only visitors had been her brother and future brother-in-law. Still in a daze, I stood up and went to look through the peephole like I'd seen Joan do. Nobody was there. Had I imagined the sound? I shook my head and headed to the kitchen to forage for more of my roommate's fantastic cookies.

A sudden odor assailed my nostrils as soon as I sat down and grabbed a cookie. The smell of sulfur, strong and acidic, burst and spread around me. I dropped the cookie onto the plate and jumped to my feet, my heart setting out in a race. Asmodeus was here.

"You've made yourself quite comfortable here, haven't you?" His rough, throaty voice was an unwelcome addition to my day. "You seem to be enjoying yourself a bit too much, I think."

Like a child caught in the act of coloring the wall of his room, I shook my head and lowered my eyes. "Asmodeus, no, not at all." I was fully aware that I sounded weak and terrified, my stomach turning in disgust. "My charge is at work, and there is nothing else I can do right now."

A wavering of the air in front of me solidified into the hated form of my dark master, impossibly tall and muscular, skin almost fully covered in tattoos that seemed to move and change every time I looked. His long dark hair was tied in the back into a half bun, half ponytail. It was his eyes, however, that were the scariest thing about him—onyx with the shine of a dying star. They seemed to devour me whole.

"So you must have news for me, then." I had nothing. Joan didn't seem to have anything extraordinary about her other than she was an amazing human. Whom I was falling in love with, whatever that meant. I hung my head even lower, bracing myself for what was surely coming. "No? Nothing? You're beginning to really piss me off, minion. And you know what happens when you piss me off." Shudders ran through me. I knew too well what he would do to me if I couldn't come up with something. Anything. The problem was I had absolutely nothing that would interest my master in any possible way. Her behavior and interaction with her brother and his fiancé the many times they had come to visit had only reinforced my belief that there was nothing unusual or remarkable about her or her family. "I'll have to plan an appropriate punishment for you. In the meantime, you stay here and keep watch. I will send another angel to take care of her."

Unwisely, I lifted my head. "What do you mean?" Stupid. So stupid. Never, ever question the master—rule one in every dark angel codebook. But this was Joan's life on the line, and for the first time in my existence, I was willing to risk it if it meant her safety.

Asmodeus's eyes darkened further, and the sulfur odor intensified. "It means, lowly angel, that she must be dealt with, something you are obviously incapable of doing."

Being dealt with could only mean one thing when it came to my master—he was planning on taking her to the Fortress, regardless of any "information" I found out about her. He wouldn't kill her because that was forbidden by celestial law, but he would play with her and her mind until she would be nothing but an empty shell of herself, incapable of thought or action. I couldn't let that happen.

"No, Master, please. Let me prove myself worthy of your trust." I didn't know where I had found the strength to talk, much less to try to fool Asmodeus. "I will take care of her myself, Master. I can do it. I want to do it."

Onyx eyes still flaring, the dark master paused, his lips tight and fingers clenched into claws, the way they were anytime he was considering the possibilities. "I like this more decisive side of you, minion. I will give you the chance to prove yourself to me." I let out the breath I'd been holding, hoping he wouldn't notice my relief. "But your punishment is coming. I'm sure I will come up with a couple of fun things to do to you." My insides cramped. What Asmodeus called fun didn't quite translate as such for me. "Don't delay. I tire of this waiting game. Do it now. I'll check on you again in a few days." The master's body became blurry as he began to vanish, but before he was totally gone, he turned to me, waved his hand in the air, and added, "Don't disappoint me."

What was I going to do? Dealing with Joan the way the dark master wanted me to was not something I could or wanted to do. My sweet human had become the most important thing in my life, the only thing that mattered. After tasting from that fountain of light, I couldn't go back to the darkness of my life. I had to come up with a plan quickly.

A glimpse at the clock told me Joan would be done at work in the next half hour or so. I put on jeans and a T-shirt, slipped into a pair of sneakers, and left the house, my wings twitching on my back, begging to unfurl. It had been a long time since I had allowed them to open completely. I had partially unfurled them once or twice when Joan was away at work, but I had an irrational fear that she'd see me and hate me for what I was, a dark angel. Now, like limbs that had been forced still for too long, they itched to be freed from the constraints of their hiding place. No time for it now though.

As I ran down the hill to the lab where Joan worked, I saw her exiting the building. The mere sight of her turned me into a warm mush. Was this love? If so, I was in so much trouble. I'd fallen in love with the one human my master hated the most at the moment.

I ran faster toward her until her eyes turned in my direction and opened wide. When I finally reached her, she seemed stunned, as if she was seeing me for the first time. There was confusion and maybe even a tad bit of fear. Fear? Why would she be afraid of me? I reached for her but she backed off, her earlier smile turned into a frown.

"You're him," she said in a whisper. I stared at her in confusion.

What did she mean? "You're the dark angel that took that soul a few months ago."

Like a punch to the stomach, I realized what Asmodeus had done to force my hand—he had removed whatever charms he had put in place for Joan not to recognize me. There was no more hiding. Joan knew I was an instrument of evil and unworthy of her love.

# CHAPTER 7

## LOVE

## JOAN

The wings were missing, and he was not as scantily dressed as the first time I saw him, but there was no mistaking that Phoenix was the same dark angel who I'd witnessed collecting the soul of the man running from the police. How was it possible I had never noticed it before? Angel magic, I was sure. Sky had told us many times that angels had ways of staying invisible to humans when they wanted to.

"What do you want from me?" I said, staying out of his reach, not sure yet how I felt about this. I didn't want to give him any opportunity to further confuse me. "Why have you been staying with me, pretending to be another human?" And how had Sky not seen through it? You'd think an angel would be able to detect another through angelic voodoo.

Phoenix looked pale and distraught. "I'm sorry, Joan. It wasn't my idea." He twisted his hands and stared down at his feet. "I'm so, so sorry, but we don't have time for explanations now. You're in danger. We have to do something."

Simmering, I lifted a hand between us. "Kind of convenient, don't you think? To have to 'save' me as soon as I find out who—what you really are." My words hit the mark. His face contorted as if I had punched him in the gut. "Tell me the truth. What are you doing here?"

His stunning hazel eyes were suspiciously shiny. Was he putting on a show to fool me into a false sense of security? "I'm telling you the truth, Joan. I will tell you all you want to know as soon as I'm sure you're safe."

I wasn't that easy to fool, or at least that's what I told myself. I had been tricked into believing he was a gentle, beautiful human. What else had he lied about? "What you may not know is that Sky, my brother's fiancé, is an angel too. One of the good ones, unlike you."

He flinched as if in pain.

"Then you know that angels have to follow orders. Unfortunately, I work for a cruel master, Joan, and he wants you," he said. Despite my resolve, a frisson of fear ran through me. "When you saw me at the accident as I plucked that soul, you unwittingly put yourself on his radar. He doesn't like that you can see angels. Asmodeus thinks you're a danger to him."

That name made me shiver from head to toe. "Asmodeus? The dark lord?"

His eyes opened wide. "You know about him?"

"Yes, of course. He's the one who gave Samael the idea to burn Sky's wings." The memory was as painful to me as back when it happened. The image of Sky curled up in bed, wings burned to stubs on his back, was too hurtful even now. "You work for the cruelest of angels?"

Phoenix nodded. "I mean you no harm, Joan, I swear," he whispered urgently. "On the contrary, I want to protect you from him."

The bitter taste of betrayal lingered on my tongue. "Wouldn't you have done that if you'd stayed away from me instead?" He nodded again, his shoulders slumped and back arched. "Then why did you do it? Why, Phoenix?" I realized I was yelling and toned it down so as not to attract attention from passersby.

"Because I am scared to death of him. He has tortured me for an eternity, Joan. He has made me weak, unable to stand up for myself or others." Even though I was sure he was lying, I flinched at the mention of torture. I had seen what that looked like up close and personal. "But that was before I knew you."

"But now you've seen the error of your ways and want to atone for it, right?" The sarcasm in my voice was so thick you could cut it with a knife.

Phoenix sighed deeply, his Adam's apple bobbing up and down. "Now, I'm stronger because of you, Joan. It's a first for me, lowly creature of darkness, to feel what I feel." He looked down briefly before raising his eyes to me again. "I'm not sure why or how, but I think I've fallen in love with you, Joan. Me, someone who doesn't even know what that is. I love you, and I don't want my master to hurt you."

The world swayed, and I had to lean against the building so I wouldn't fall. What had he just said? He loved me? Could angels of the dark love anyone or anything? And was he being honest or saying what he thought I wanted to hear? After all, he couldn't have missed the fact that I wanted him. Badly.

"Please, Jo. You can call your brother and his fiancé, whatever you need to do, but we have to move quickly. Asmodeus thinks I'm taking care of the problem myself. When I don't bring you back to the Fortress, he'll be back, and he will be pissed. Never a good idea to piss the dark lord off." He spoke fast, not pausing between sentences. "Please, Jo, I'm begging you."

Why did he have to use the nickname he'd given me? Something inside melted, and I wanted to believe him. "Let me call Sky." That was the only thing I could do, since I had no other way of knowing whether Phoenix was telling the truth. I pulled the phone from my jeans pocket and punched Sky's number.

He answered right away. "What's wrong, Joan? I had a bad premonition." Tarnation. This angelic shit was very real. "What's going on? Where are you?"

"Take a breather, Sky," I said lightly, trying not to spook him. "I'm fine. I have a question for you though."

I could almost see my angel friend relax, his muscles and blue eyes softening. "Sure, what is it?"

"Can dark angels love?"

"What? Joan, what is going on?" He was in a panic now. Damn, exactly what I was trying to avoid.

"Relax, Sky. It's a simple question."

To my utter surprise, Phoenix took the phone from me and addressed Sky directly. "Sky, I'm a dark angel, sent to Earth by Asmodeus to spy on Joan," he said, and I could hear the gasps from the other end of the line. "She's in danger, Sky. Asmodeus wants to take her to the Fortress. I need to make sure he doesn't."

There was silence, and I watched Phoenix closely as he absorbed whatever Sky was telling him, licked his lips, and then gazed into my eyes. "Why? Because I love her, Sky. I love Joan."

✝

## NIX

I couldn't understand how I didn't see it before. Maybe the fact that he had lost his wings made him less recognizable as the angel he was, or maybe I had lost my ability to identify other angelic creatures. Sky told us to stay put and that he was coming over as fast as he could—which was pretty fast, considering he was using prosthetic wings.

"I haven't said anything to Caleb yet," he said as soon as he alit in our backyard. His wings might not have been natural, but they were still magnificent, snow white with a silvery hint around each perfect feather. Despite the gravity of our situation, I couldn't help but admire the amazing workmanship that went into building something that intricate. "I didn't want him to worry himself sick at work."

"She won't listen to me," I complained, a note of irritation in my voice. "Maybe she'll listen to you."

Sky stared me down. "I knew there was something about you, but I couldn't put my finger on it." He turned to Joan, who had parked herself stubbornly on the couch, a scowl on her face. "How can you be sure he's the angel you saw, Joan? For that matter, how can you be sure he's an angel at all?"

To speed things up, I unfurled my wings, almost knocking down a flower pot on the small coffee table and a framed print from the wall. I heard Joan gasp as she took in my raven-black wings, extended to their widest span. "Yes, I am an angel," I said unnecessarily. "And she's right—I am the angel she saw at the accident site."

"What have you been doing here all along? Did you mean her harm?" Sky's usual smile had been replaced by an angry frown. "I should call the Council of Archangels and report you. Hurting humans is forbidden." He would know, since the angelic laws had been amended because of what had happened to him.

"I was—am not here to hurt Joan. At first, I was to spy on her and try to figure out why she could see me and then report to my master," I explained, fully aware they doubted every word I uttered. "But he has run out of patience, as he often does, and now he wants to make sure she's not a threat."

Joan, who had been quiet for the whole conversation, uncrossed her arms and said, "Like I really would be a threat to the angels. I have no powers or magic."

I sighed. "This is Asmodeus we're talking about. He feels threatened by the wind, and he's always excited about getting new pawns for his unsavory games." I knew that fact intimately. "He will be here in the next few days, and he will take you away, Joan." I lowered my voice to a whisper. "I can't let that happen. I can't."

Even though I was staring at my feet, I could feel the intensity of Sky's stare burning my skin. "What do you propose we do? And why should we trust you?"

"We need to hide Joan somewhere safe first," I said, not sure where that safe place might be. "Then I will wait for Asmodeus and tell him I don't know where she is."

Sky's sudden intake of air made me look at him again. "He will kill you. Worse, he'll torture you for all eternity." Yes, in a nutshell. "Why would you do that for Joan?"

I stole a quick glance in her direction before hiding my eyes again. "I told you already. I've fallen in love with her."

Silence fell, a heavy curtain that muffled every other noise. I didn't dare look up, afraid of what I might read on their faces. How did I, an angel of darkness, dare love a human? What right did I have to love at all?

Sky's voice was soft and warm. "How do you know you love her? Have you ever loved anyone before?"

I wished I knew the answer. "Not that I can remember," I admitted. "Not that I remember much of my life before—" My voice caught, and I took a breath and swallowed the lump in my throat. "But I seem to remember this feeling, an overwhelming feeling of warmth and yearning, of caring about someone else, of wanting to protect her and do everything in my power to make her happy. I don't know how I know this is love, I just do."

I peeked at Joan from the corner of my eye and was immediately mesmerized by her expression. She looked like a star in the night sky, her face lit up and her eyes shiny with emotion. I could not let my master mar such pure beauty.

"No." Joan's exclamation took me and Sky by surprise. We both looked at her in disbelief. What did she mean? "I will not let you sacrifice yourself for me, Nix. I may be pissed at you right now, but I would never allow anyone to put himself in that position."

"But, Joan, if Asmodeus gets to you—" Sky couldn't finish. Joan lifted a hand and shook her head. "Tarnation, girl. Why do you have to be so stubborn?"

Joan smiled that little mischievous smile of hers. "That's why you love me, Sky." I couldn't be sure what she meant by that, the subtleties of human repartee still a bit of a mystery to me, but I wanted to have someone who'd feel comfortable enough to talk to me that way too.

Sky turned to me. "Since the lady here won't listen to common sense, this is what we will do," he said. "I will contact Gabriel and see what he can do, and in the meantime, I will leave you in charge, Phoenix." Joan opened her mouth, but it was Sky's turn to lift a hand to stop her. "Not a word, girl. You know as well as I do that angels have powers that humans don't. You couldn't stand up to

Asmodeus or any of his minions if you were the strongest weight lifter in the world."

I cringed. I was one of those minions. Except I had no intention of following my master's commands.

Joan groaned and stomped her foot. "You are worse than my brother." Was that a good or bad thing? It was hard to tell. Despite the emphatic groan, Joan had a tiny smile playing in the corner of her lips. "Okay, I'll stay put and let Nix be my guardian angel."

Her words had the effect of a blast. The world wavered around me, my eyes unable to focus on anything and my stomach threatening to empty itself. I fell to my knees, a sense of overwhelming sadness filling me.

Joan ran to my side and kneeled beside me. "What's wrong?"

I couldn't answer. Not only was I tongue-tied with a sudden tidal wave of emotion, but I didn't know the cause for such reaction. My body seemed to remember, but I had no such knowledge. Why had Joan's words affected me so much?

"Nix, what's going on? You're as pale as a ghost." Joan was still by my side, her arm over my shoulder, holding me against her. Unshed tears choked me, but I didn't want her to see that. I hung my head, hiding my eyes and blocking her from seeing my trembling lips. What was wrong with me? Had my unconscious self recalled something I couldn't?

I gave in to her warmth and leaned against her, a wave of comfort and relief running through me at the contact. Loving this tiny woman was either going to be my salvation or my final unraveling.

# JOAN

I paced the floor outside his room. Behind the closed door, Sky was checking on Phoenix, and I was anxious to find out what had happened. One minute he was standing, looking bewildered as he often did, and the next he was on the floor, pale and shaking. Sky had immediately carried him—I was still in awe of how strong angels were—to his room and slammed the door shut behind him.

I touched my ear to the door, trying to listen in, but no sounds came through. What had I said to cause that reaction? Or did he just get sick suddenly? Did angels get sick? I couldn't recall Sky ever being sick, not even when his wings had been savagely burned by Samael. Was it some weird angel condition I was not aware of?

The lock clicked and I stepped away as the door opened. Sky came out, closing the door behind him again.

"Well, what's wrong?" I asked, seeking some kind of answer in his expression. "What's going on with Nix?"

Sky slid an arm over my shoulders. "He's fine." That was not what fine looked like. "Something you said triggered a memory."

"Since when are memories powerful enough to knock someone down like that?" I hated feeling lost.

"I can't be sure, but it looks as if his memories were erased," Sky said, leading me to the couch. "Sometimes when something happens that the dark masters don't want their servants to remember, they wipe their memories. Actually, angels of light do that too. Gabriel wiped Caleb's memory of me after we met for the first time, remember?"

I pulled my legs up and curled them beneath me. "But that was only one memory. He doesn't seem to remember much of anything."

"Yes, it's strange. I don't know enough about the dark angels to be able to explain it." Sky pecked my cheek. "For what it's worth, I do believe him." I stared at him and blinked. "I believe that he has fallen in love with you. Asmodeus is not the kind of angel you want to piss off, and yet, Phoenix is willing to risk it to protect you."

That didn't make me feel any better. I was developing feelings for him too, and I definitely didn't want him to put himself in harm's way to shelter me. I could take care of myself, even though going against an evil angel might be a little out of my comfort zone.

"Can you help him? He seemed so distressed after I joked about him being my guardian angel." I guess I didn't want to admit to myself that I was worried sick about Phoenix. I had seen what a dark angel could do. The thought that what happened to Sky could happen to my angel made me sick to my stomach.

Wait! When did I start thinking of Phoenix as my angel?

Sky let out a deep sigh. "I will talk to Gabriel and see if he has any insights into this." He slid off the couch and onto his feet as gracefully as a cat. "He's not going to be too happy about this, I'll tell you that. And, Joan, I have to tell your brother." I opened my mouth to protest, but he interrupted me. "I have to. He would never forgive me if something happened to you on my watch."

Oh boy. He'd fuss and worry himself raw, which meant endless phone calls and visits that would drive me crazy. I could hear him already. "No, you won't go to work, girl. It's dangerous." I loved my brother, but he could be such an old man sometimes.

Sky left after instructing me to let Phoenix rest for a while. Sky had given him some weird angelic remedy so he could relax. "We don't sleep much, but he needs it right now. Let him sleep for another hour or so." I obliged. I needed time to get my own thoughts and feelings in order.

As per my normal, I baked cookies while pondering over the whole Phoenix conundrum. How did I feel about him exactly? I was attracted to him. Check. I was seriously hot for him. Check. I was falling for the fallen angel. I scooped the batter from the bowl with an ice cream scoop and began dropping the raw cookies onto the pan. Was I falling for Phoenix? Or was it just lust? The truth was Phoenix was a manly work of sexy art, and any woman who claimed to not be attracted to him was a flat-out liar, but was I falling in love with him? The other question was, did I need that kind of complication in my life right now? Any relationship would be a stumbling block in my current professional track, but one with an angel was insane.

Why were our lives so entangled with the paranormal world of the angels? Since both my brother and I had seen the angel who'd come to collect our parents' souls after the accident, our world had become connected with the heavenly creatures.

There were still no sounds of life crossing the thin wood of Phoenix's door, so I put all my doubts aside and went in to see him.

I didn't make it too far into the room. He was lying on his back, no shirt, his beautiful dark wings still unfurled under him, framing him like a beautiful piece of art. With one hand resting on his belly, raven-black hair and olive skin, Phoenix was a masterpiece.

*Oh shit. I am falling for him.*

Yes, I wanted to run to him, strip him of the rest of his clothes, and make mad, passionate love to him. But I also wanted to run my fingers through his hair, pull his face to my shoulder, and erase his pain. I felt so much more than just lust.

He stirred, awakened by my presence—and probably by my heavy breathing. His eyes searched my face until he found mine. He held my gaze silently before speaking. "I'm sorry, Joan. I wish I could change things."

I couldn't help it. "You wish you didn't fall in love with me?"

He sat up, leaning on his elbows. "No. I wish I was worthy of you, Jo," he said. "I wish I wasn't who—what I am. I wish you could love me back."

Something burst inside of me and flooded my heart with such love, I thought I'd explode. "You fool," I said, my voice cracking with emotion. "I don't care who you are. I'm falling for you too. So hard, I may never get up again."

Phoenix blinked, his luscious lips parted. "Yes?"

Tired of resisting the urge, I flew forward and jumped on the bed, throwing myself in his arms. He lost his balance and dropped flat on the pillow, laughing. "Yes, fuck yes. I'm smitten, my sweet, gorgeous angel." I wrapped my arms around his neck and pulled him

## NIX

For a moment I thought I was dreaming. Angels didn't dream often, but it wasn't unheard of. Joan had thrown herself in my arms and linked her lips to mine in a kiss that left me breathless and wanting more. "W-Wait," I stuttered, pulling her away enough to look her in the eye. "What did you say?"

"I like your wings." She gave me a devilish smile, and my insides liquefied.

"No, before that. Did you say you were falling for me?" I wasn't sure I had heard her correctly. "Because I thought I heard you—"

She shut me up with another ferocious kiss. Was that a yes?

For a human, Joan had an astonishing capability to go without breathing for a long time. I was the one gasping for air as our lips finally parted, but maybe that had nothing to do with breathing and everything to do with the fact that her kiss made my blood run through me faster than an angelic messenger.

"I'm not ready to confirm or deny that," she said, her serious expression turning into a wicked smile. She exploded laughing. I was confused, as usual. Obviously she said something funny, but I had nothing to connect the words with, so I attempted a smile. She laughed harder. "Oh, sweet angel, I'll have to teach you a thing or two."

I had no problem with that.

Like a few days before, Joan began peeling clothes off me, dragging my pants over my hips, my thighs, carelessly to the floor. Straddling my legs, she studied me with hunger in her eyes. "Can I touch you?" At first, I was surprised by the request, then remembered what had happened the first time we were in that same situation, so I nodded. "I don't want to do anything you don't want me to do."

I swallowed. It had to be said. I couldn't keep secrets from Joan. If she was going to trust me with her life, I had to trust her with mine. "Asmodeus makes me beg for mercy when he uses me," I whispered, a flutter of doubt in my chest. "It's more fun for him that way."

Joan's mouth opened but no sound came out. She sat back on my thighs, her hands burning pleasantly on my hips. "What?"

I was committed to the truth now. "When you said those words, memories of my encounters with the dark lord flooded my mind."

"He raped you?"

I had never thought of it that way. As a dark angel, I was supposed to serve my master any way he saw fit. Asmodeus was creative with his demands. If one day all he wanted me to do was bring him fresh souls, and the next he wanted me in his chambers, naked and vulnerable, ready for his perverse kind of plucking, as much as I hated it, it was my duty to obey, to submit.

"The fucker! Let me have a word with that motherfu—"

I sat up suddenly and wrapped my hands around her, quieting her with my lips. She shook against me but relaxed after a while, her muscles softening as our kiss deepened.

"I told you because I want you to trust me as I trust you," I whispered in her ear, her head resting on my shoulder. "In my world, it's not illegal or frowned upon. Each master disciplines his or her angels however they want. It's everyday life for us dark angels."

Her lips were playing havoc with my senses as she dropped kisses on my neck and shoulder. "Have you ever had…?"

I knew what she meant. "Pleasant sex?" I searched for the right answer, but my muddled memories wouldn't allow me much clarity. "I think so. I seem to recall it, but I couldn't tell you when or how or with whom."

Joan was quiet for a while, her lips still lingering on the crook of my neck. I couldn't see her face, and I wondered whether I had spooked her with my story of angelic woes. The tone of her voice had spoken volumes—shock, maybe pity. I didn't want her to pity me. I knew I was weak, a worthless pawn in my master's games, spineless and helpless, but I didn't want her to think of me that way. My heart wished she could see me as the angel she deserved, not this sorry excuse for a heavenly creature.

"Can I show you?" She had been silent for so long, I was surprised by her question.

"Show me what?" *Please, God, don't let her hate me. Anything but that.*

Her hand slid down my arm until she wove her fingers with mine. "Can I show you how wonderful sex can be? No, can I show you what making love looks and feels like?"

I was speechless. Did that mean she didn't think badly of me? The ways of humans still confused me most of the time, but her gentle voice told me she was not repulsed by me. I nodded, incapable of speaking and not sure of what I really wanted. My only certainty was my growing love for Joan. The rest was a vast unknown.

Letting go of my hand, she brushed her fingers along the edge of one of my wings in a soft caress. My dark feathers fanned and stirred at her touch, and I was surprised to find my body also responding to her. Instead of the fear that always overcame me when my master touched me, pleasure ran through me and I swelled.

She lifted her face to look at me and smiled. "Does it feel good when I touch your feathers?" Her fingers continued their track over my wing, making me shiver in delight.

I tried to speak, but the words wouldn't leave my mouth. Heat was covering my skin from head to toe as an irresistible wish to draw her into my arms and kiss her again threatened to explode.

She stopped me from pulling her closer, and for a second I thought I had done something wrong. But then I saw her smile and I knew everything was all right. There was a promise in her eyes that I couldn't wait to unravel.

## JOAN

For once I was glad my libido was overriding my rational thoughts. If I had a moment to think about Phoenix's revelations, I would either be sick or burst in anger. A thought for a later time. The moment was filled with my dark angel and how he felt underneath me, his tanned skin almost shining as I took my time touching every inch of him. At my request, he had not retracted his enormous black wings, beautiful and soft, a hint of blue under the feathers. Silly as it was, they made me want him even more. I had possibly lost my mind. Joan, the never-attached, career-oriented woman who now wanted nothing else but to be with that creature of the night.

"Tell me if I make you uncomfortable," I told him, spreading my hands over his belly and sliding them up to his hairless chest. A whimper of satisfaction escaped my lips when I felt him tremble. "Do you want me to stop?"

Phoenix smiled and shook his head. "I trust you."

Those three little words made my heart swell and my hormones run wild. What could be sexier than a man who trusted you implicitly?

I scooted up until I was sitting over his hips. His hardness rubbed against my jeans and I melted. Damn clothes! But I wanted this to be all about him. Now that he had allowed me a glimpse into his life in what he called the Fortress, I wanted to make him feel good in a wholesome, loving way. I wanted, more than anything else, to show him what love could be like, that he was worthy of being loved.

Leaning over him, I kissed and ran my tongue over his chest, lingering over the spots that made him quiver. Then I slid down again until I could taste him fully. So engrossed in the feelings that this angel stirred in me, I didn't stop to wonder why I felt so at ease doing something I had never done before.

He pressed his lower body against my mouth, groaning softly, and I chanced a quick glance at him. His hands were clenched on the sheets, knuckles white, eyes closed as his chin tilted up, the arch of his back hovering over the bed as if he were taking flight. A crazy thought crossed my mind—how amazing it would be to make love while flying. Was that even possible? Yes, obviously I had totally lost my mind.

I inched my hands underneath him to clutch the hard mounds of his bottom while another insane thought assailed me—could angels manipulate your mind so you'd do what they wanted? I had never been this wanton, this feverishly driven by desire. Was it the magnetic attraction between us or some angelic voodoo? I decided I didn't care. It was wild and all-encompassing, my whole body coming alive and he hadn't even touched me yet. The mere thought of his hands and his mouth on me almost made me come undone.

Without warning, Phoenix pulled me away from him, and with a swift, fluid move, he flipped us so I was now underneath him, trembling in anticipation. Phoenix's powerful wings provided a shelter from the room around us, creating the illusion of a world of our own. His mouth descended on mine and pried my lips open, his tongue teasingly inviting mine for a dance. I moaned against his lips, wanting to swallow him whole.

"Take my clothes off, Nix." It was an urgent plea. I was not sure how much longer I could last before my muscles released all that thrilling, overwhelming pressure we were creating.

Phoenix hesitated for a second before pulling my T-shirt over my head. I arched my back so he could reach around me and unfasten my bra. The cool air blew over my bare breasts, making them tingle and then blaze as he latched his mouth around one of them, his tongue teasing a spiraling storm of pleasure in me.

With a wiggle, I helped him remove my jeans and my panties until I was finally as gloriously naked as he was. Phoenix studied me, hazel eyes hidden behind his thick lashes and swollen lips slightly parted.

"I didn't know it could be like this," he whispered, his body propped up on his arms. "I love you, Jo." He lowered himself on top of me and retracted his wings, the wondrous feathers disappearing with a quiet swoosh into his back. I wanted to complain, but I was too distracted by what the contact with his body was doing to mine.

I wrapped my leg around his hips, resting my foot on his back, and held my breath as he eased his length inside me. I gasped and pressed myself closer to him. I heard him moan, his face buried in the crook of my neck, and for a moment I worried. Was he okay? Was this too much for him? *Oh God, let this not bring bad memories to him.* But a moment later, he raised his head to gaze into my eyes. Shit. I was definitely falling in love with him.

Phoenix looked at me again as if asking for permission to proceed. I nodded and brushed my hand across his chest. He leaned closer and kissed me before beginning an ebb-and-flow dance that carried me all the way up to the sky, where I exploded into a million stars. I pressed him closer and heard him grunt, his body trembling against mine, giving in to the pleasure we had conjured. For an insane moment, I could have sworn his skin was shimmering.

A scream of pure ecstasy reached my ears, and it took me a while to realize it was mine. Phoenix was the silent type apparently, voicing his pleasure with soft grunts and moans even when he reached his climax shortly after me. I held him tight, not wanting to be separated from him, enjoying the incredible sense of intimacy our body contact created. It wasn't until he slid out of me that it hit me—we hadn't used a condom. Stupid girl. I knew better than that.

Sensing my sudden distress, Phoenix, now lying beside me, held my gaze with his. "What's wrong?" He sounded pained, almost panicky. "Did I do it wrong? Did I hurt you?"

I almost laughed at the ridiculousness of his question. He had done nothing wrong, and hell no, he hadn't hurt me in any way, as my still-tingling skin could attest. "No, it's not that, Nix," I rushed to clarify. "I forgot to use a condom. After all, we barely know each other."

Phoenix gave that birdlike head-tilt look. "Condom? What's that?" I couldn't believe I had to explain such a basic thing to a creature who was much, much older than me, if Sky was anything to go by. I did my best to state it in layman's terms. His eyes opened wide as I explained the prophylactic role in preventing certain diseases and unwanted pregnancies. He smiled. "Angels don't carry diseases, and I'm pretty sure we can't procreate with humans." His "pretty sure" statement didn't do much to appease my qualms, but it was better than nothing, especially since now it was too late to do anything about it.

I pulled my thoughts away from the vexing subject and focused on my roommate, gorgeously naked beside me. "How was it?" As cheesy as the question was, I had to ask after what he had told me about his previous experiences with sex.

The smile that spread across his lips was all the answer I needed. I leaned forward and kissed him, unable to resist the weird but lovely yearning in my gut.

Oh, fuck! I was in so much trouble.

# CHAPTER 8
## THE PLAN

## NIX

The rays of light sneaked in through the gaps in the curtains, and reality hit me like a meteor. Here I was, lying next to this tiny human, my heart full of a feeling I had never felt before, and ignoring the fact that Asmodeus would be coming back soon to take her away from me. I had to figure something out. Quickly.

"Why the long face?" Joan was awake, staring up at me, her hand playfully skimming my thigh.

"Asmodeus will come. We need a plan." Her hand distracted me, muddling my thoughts. "Jo, we have to do something. You have no idea how cruel he is."

Joan stopped moving her hand and propped herself up. "I certainly do. He's the one who cheered Samael and provided him with the weapon to torture and burn Sky's wings. I do know. I just refuse to be terrified." I was. Scared stiff. "Sky said he would get Gabriel involved."

"The archangel? You've met him?" Joan never ceased to amaze me. For a mere mortal, she sure had some high connections in the angelic world. Then again, she wasn't just a mortal, was she? There was something special and magical about my girl. Wait! Was I allowed to think of her as mine? Not in the possessive, material sort of way, but mine to keep in my heart forever.

"He loves my cookies," she said cryptically with a laugh. "Don't be surprised if he pops out of nowhere. He gives me the creeps, but he's our best chance at dealing with the angelic asshole."

"Why would he help me? I'm on the other side." I had absolutely zero faith that an archangel would be willing to lend a hand against Asmodeus, a force to be reckoned with on either side of the heavenly world.

With a sigh, Joan cupped my cheek with her hand and smiled. "Of course he will. I can perform miracles with my cookies." Could she really, or was she joking? I still found it hard to tell. I was about to ask her when she reached out and took my lips with hers, effectively wiping any other thought I might have had. Her taste was intoxicating and addictive. I didn't want her to stop her teasing tongue rubbing against mine.

Reality interrupted us in the form of the loud ringing of a phone. She pulled away and reached out for the phone lying on the nightstand. "It's my brother," she said, pressing a key on the device. "Hey, Caleb. What's up?"

I sat up, scooting all the way until my back was against the wooden headboard, watching her. With the phone in her hand, Joan curled her legs underneath her, and I felt the stirring of desire again. She was perfect—her freckled face framed by her dark hair, the small rounded mounds of her breasts, her narrow hips and well-shaped legs. Perfection in a tiny frame.

"Don't give me that shit, Caleb. I'm not a fucking child anymore." The conversation didn't seem to be going too well. Joan had that tightness on her lips I had come to identify with anger and frustration. "I will do as I please, bro. You're not my father." She quieted down for a moment, listening to whatever her brother was telling her from the other end. I could listen in if I wanted to, my angel ears well built for eavesdropping, but I didn't feel I should interfere. "Okay, that's fine. I'll be waiting."

"What happened?" She had set the phone back on the nightstand. "Is everything all right with your brother and Sky?"

"Gabriel is coming," she said, jumping out of bed and picking up her discarded clothes from the floor. "We better get dressed. Something tells me he won't approve of the two of us in bed together."

Not sure of why the archangel would care whether we were in bed or not, I reluctantly got up and dressed, all the while watching Joan as she slipped into one piece of clothing at a time, the cloth rubbing against her satiny skin. Before I knew it, my body was reacting to her again. I almost asked her if we could get under the sheets and recreate what we had done earlier, but I knew this meeting with Gabriel was important, so I bit my lip and stationed my gaze on the floor instead.

We were barely finished when the sound of a gruff voice echoed through the house. "Fuck. He's here." Neglecting to put on shoes, Joan swung the door open and left me alone in the room. A sense of fear came out of nowhere and settled in my stomach. Why would I be scared of meeting the archangel? He had no jurisdiction over my kind, yet the butterflies of anxiety had invaded my insides. I had to force myself to follow Joan.

"I made these especially for you," I heard Joan say in a honeyed voice that didn't quite fit her. "I know how much you love them."

The cranky voice I had heard before said, "Don't try to bribe me, young woman. Bribes don't work with the archangels." But his voice betrayed a note of gentleness nevertheless.

Joan was busy arranging some of her cookies on a plate when I walked in the kitchen. Gabriel was standing with his back turned to me. He was tall and looked a lot younger than what I thought he ought to look, considering he was more than a thousand years old. I supposed I'd imagined him as an old decrepit angel, hunched back and gnarled fingers, but I should have known better—there was no ugliness in the angelic world. At least not in the physical sense of the term.

Joan looked up at me, her eyes shiny with mischief. "Oh, there you are, Nix. Come and meet Gabriel."

The archangel turned, and I was nearly knocked to my knees. I had never seen him before—angels of light didn't associate with those of the dark—but something distressingly familiar punched my breath out of me. I gasped as his intense blue eyes met mine and a new wave of fear, stronger than the first, made its way through me. Gabriel flinched as if he too had recognized me in some way.

"Gabriel, this is Phoenix, my angelic roommate." Joan had walked over, her eyebrows curved into an arch and her eyes ping-ponging between the two of us. So she had noticed the tension too. "We both need your help."

The older angel shook his head and took a bite of his cookie, disguising his obvious discomfort. My breath was coming out in spurts, and I had to grab the wall so I wouldn't fall. What was this? Why did I feel as if I knew this angel when I didn't? Had I met him a long time ago, before my memory had gone blank? And if so, why was I afraid of him? He was an archangel, a divine being of light, pledged to the good, not evil like Asmodeus. Not someone I should be afraid of, surely.

After a moment of awkwardness, Gabriel swallowed the cookie and extended his hand to me. "Nice to meet you, Phoenix. I hear you're trying to do the right thing." That was a strange thing to say, however true.

I shook his hand, a slight tremor betraying my smile. "Nice to meet you, Archangel. It's an honor."

Gabriel removed his hand from mine a tad too quickly and coughed. "No need for formality here," he said, smile gone. "Let's talk about your situation, shall we?"

We all sat in the living room, Joan's thigh glued to mine, offering me a measure of comfort and support I should've been giving her instead. She had brought the plate with the cookies with her and placed it beside the archangel's chair, a clear attempt at appeasing him.

"We're in a pickle, Gabriel," she said, her hand seeking mine on my lap. She threaded her fingers through mine, and I held on tight. "Phoenix wants to protect me by finding a place to hide me and then be the sacrificial lamb. I do not want to be taken by the dark lord, but I also don't want Nix to suffer for me."

Gabriel swallowed hard and avoided my eyes. "It is indeed a tricky situation, Joan." He grabbed the glass of milk Joan had placed next to the cookies and gulped down at least half of it. "The problem is I don't have jurisdiction in the dark side, you see. Yes, I can do something about angelic laws being broken, but according to what Sky told me, no laws have been broken as yet."

I bristled. "Are you telling me that Asmodeus must first take Joan to the Fortress before you can do anything about it?" It was not wise to raise your voice at an archangel, but I couldn't help it. "By the time you get to her, she would have already gone through hell. You know how cruel Asmodeus is. He won't lose any time breaking her apart before you can stop him."

Gabriel raised a hand. "I didn't say we wouldn't do anything. I said it was tricky." He looked at Joan's hand connected with mine and sighed. "What's with angels falling for mortals lately?" he exclaimed. "Not a wise thing at all."

"Don't deflect, Gabriel," Joan said, scooting closer to the edge of the couch. "Our relationship or lack thereof has nothing to do with this. The question is, what can we do to keep me from being tortured by the not-so-lovely prince of darkness while keeping Nix safe and sound?"

Silence fell. Gabriel retreated into himself in thought. We both waited, but before he could say anything, a knock on the door interrupted him.

Caleb and Sky entered the house without waiting for anyone to open the door; the angel hadn't lost all his skills after all. Caleb immediately fell to his knees by Joan and wrapped her in a hug. "Stupid girl, why are you always in trouble?" he said, his voice muffled. "Shit, I thought that now that you're an adult, I wouldn't have to worry so much about you."

Joan slapped him playfully and pulled him away. "Stop that, Caleb. I'm not a child anymore." Her hand was still holding mine, a fact that didn't escape her brother's attention. "We'll figure something out. We always do."

Caleb shook his head and stood up, looking at Gabriel. "So, angel, what are you going to do about this?"

It was not so much Gabriel's answer that made me shake from head to toe but the expression of loss on his face. Was I really such a lost cause after all?

✝

## JOAN

Angels were strange creatures. Beautiful and perfect in physical terms, but not so perfect inside, as I'd learned since meeting Sky.

Angels followed a strict code of rules that didn't always serve their main purpose, to spread love among humans. Angels of dark had a different purpose, of course, but even those of light often screwed up big-time. Sky was living proof of those flaws. He had been framed for a crime he didn't commit—another angel of light had, and for the most basic of human sins, jealousy and greed. The fact that Sky had asked Gabriel to join him in the kitchen for a private talk didn't leave me with a warm, fuzzy feeling.

Caleb was engrossed in conversation—more like interrogation—with Phoenix, who he now regarded as a potential threat to his baby sister, so I inched my way closer to the kitchen to eavesdrop on the conversation between the two angels. They were whispering, and I thanked my super hearing—finally honed through years of being nosy—which allowed me to hear enough of it.

"What do you mean, it's difficult? Joan is in danger, and she won't back down unless we manage to protect the angel too." Sky's voice had an irritated edge to it, not a usual thing for him at all.

"Protecting the girl is not a problem, but the angel…."

What was he talking about? He was one of the archangels, for God's sake. There wasn't much he couldn't do.

"Why can't we protect Phoenix? I know he's a dark angel, but he's trying to do the right thing." Sky's raised voice reached me easily. "Isn't that what we are all about? Helping others? Spreading the love among those who most need it? That angel needs it now."

Mumbling followed, and I stepped closer to the doorway. "…his past. We can't undo it, Sky. There are rules in place."

"What about his past, Gabriel? He doesn't even remember it." I heard pacing and the sound of chewing. Gabriel was still trying to hide behind the cookies. "Do you know something you're not telling me?"

Now, that was new and interesting. I focused my whole attention to the conversation in the kitchen, blocking the sound of my brother's and Phoenix's voices in the background.

"Yes, I remember him clearly." Gabriel's statement almost knocked me off my feet. "There was an incident many years back, before your own problem started. There's not much I can do for him. He was convicted, and you know as well as I do that's the end of the road for an angel."

Sky slapped his hand on the tabletop in an uncharacteristic show of frustration and anger. "Tarnation, Gabriel. You were able to help me. You can help him too."

"You were framed, Sky. He wasn't." What did that mean? What had Phoenix been convicted of? Even as a dark angel, he was sweet and gentle. What could he have done that was so bad? "Crimes such as his are never forgiven."

My heart dropped a few inches. No, I refused to believe that Phoenix had committed a heinous enough crime to be exiled to the dark side forever. There had to be another explanation. There had to be.

"We can still argue that he is redeeming himself now," Sky went on, not willing to give up on a fellow angel. "There must be something we can do for him, Gabriel. We can't hand him to

Asmodeus on a silver platter. The dark lord will break him, over and over again. He's one of us, an immortal. Are you really going to sit and watch a fellow angel suffer for eternity for a sin he is obviously not even aware of?"

There was silence for a few seconds. "His memories have been wiped for his own good," Gabriel said. "He doesn't remember what he did because we extended him that small kindness. His existence would be so much worse if he remembered what happened."

Sky exploded. "Have you lost your mind? How can he ever redeem himself for whatever it was he did if you won't allow him to remember it? That's not only unfair, it's cruel. I can understand it coming from Asmodeus, but from an angel of light?"

Gabriel tried to calm Sky down, shushing him. "The Council of Archangels met and made the decision together. Not all of us agreed, but the majority won. The matter was then passed on to the higher court of the Cherubim." It was not clear whether he was one who had disagreed. "But it's done, and it cannot be undone, Sky. He's on his own."

In anger, I kicked the wall, giving my presence away, and they both lowered their voices to whispers so the rest of the conversation was lost to me. Damn it! Gabriel was not going to help him. And I refused to let Asmodeus have my angel. Obviously I was no match for the dark lord, but I had to come up with something. Anything.

"Promise me you'll do whatever it takes to protect my sister," I heard Caleb say to Phoenix as I gave up my listening post and approached the couch.

Phoenix brought a hand to his chest. "With my life, if necessary."

"No you won't," I exclaimed, furious with my brother for coaxing him into making such a promise. "No one needs to put their lives on the line for me. We'll figure this out." I glared at Caleb, who glared back. "And you, my brother, stay out of my life. I love you, but I am an adult, and I prefer if you don't butt in all the time."

Caleb was not impressed by my bravado. He knew too well that as much as he drove me crazy sometimes, I would never want to live away from him or have him not meddle in my life. We had gone through too much together with our parents' accident and then his brushes with death. We were a team, come rain or shine, angels from heaven or apocalyptic lords of darkness.

"Sis, I want both of you to be safe," he said, stealing a glance at Phoenix, whose eyes were stuck to the floor, his back hunched over. "But if it comes to it, Phoenix is a lot better equipped to stand up to another angel than you will ever be. He knows that."

Yes. He also knew what kind of horrors would wait for him at the hands of his master.

I dropped by Phoenix's side and looped my arm through his. "Nix and I will have a plan in place before it comes to any of that." I sounded a lot surer than I was. "We're a couple now, and couples stick together through thick and thin, right? Didn't you do that with Sky?" Had I just committed to a relationship? *Who are you and what have you done with my true self?*

Caleb opened his mouth but said nothing. It was only then that I realized Phoenix had been quiet through the whole exchange; that worried me more than anything else right then. He had withdrawn further into himself, his body tight and still. Had I said something I shouldn't have?

Sky and Gabriel came back from the kitchen looking suspiciously chirpy. Gabriel was never chirpy.

"Drop the act, will you?" I barked at them, furious with the knowledge that the archangel refused to help Phoenix. "I can't believe you won't help another angel."

Sky coughed and hid a frown behind his hand. He too was angry at Gabriel. Dark or not, Phoenix was one of their own.

"Child, there is not much I can do for him, unfortunately." Gabriel dropped the fake smile and scowled, the cranky angel returning.

"Can't or won't?" I was not going to let him get away with it. I pounced to my feet and yanked the plate of cookies from his hand. "I won't bake for someone who refuses to help a fellow angel."

Gabriel winced, his hand still hovering midair as if holding the plate. "Child, we have rules we must follow."

"Fuck the rules, Gabriel!" Anger had exploded from inside of me and overflowed out of my mouth. "You, an angel who professes to uphold love above all else, are going to let the dark lord torture Phoenix for eternity? What kind of angel are you?"

The archangel's ivory skin flushed pink, his hands clenched into fists along his sides. "I'm not 'letting' Asmodeus do anything. Once Phoenix was convicted of his crime, I lost all authority over his fate." Phoenix snapped his head up to stare at Gabriel, who belatedly realized he had given away more information than he probably wanted. "What I mean is I don't—"

Phoenix didn't let him finish. "Crime I have committed? You know my past?" If a moment ago he had been spiritually absent, he was now animated and alert. "Why can't I remember anything? What did I do?"

Convinced that Gabriel was going to vanish in order to not answer any questions, I held on to his arm and hoped that was enough to anchor him to Earth and my living room. "Answer Nix. He deserves an answer," I told him in a low growl.

Discomfited, Gabriel sputtered sounds for a while before putting whole sentences together. "I can't tell you. This was the council's decision, not mine. And memories, once erased, can't be recovered unless it happens naturally." He sighed and lowered his voice. "I'm sorry, angel. There isn't a thing I can do for you right now."

Breathing hard, Phoenix took a moment. For the next couple heartbeats, he merely stared at me, a glint of something I couldn't identify in his eyes. When he spoke again, his breathing had slowed down and his voice was calm and in control. "You can't help me, but what about Joan? Can you do something for her?"

I couldn't believe it. Even now, after all the shocking revelations about his past and his fate, he was still putting me first. In that moment I was sure—I loved that angel, and no force on Earth or beyond was going to stop me from keeping him safe and sound in my arms.

# NIX

Caleb had taken Joan into the bedroom under much protesting. He knew I needed to iron out a few things with the archangel and Sky, and I didn't need the distraction and pressure of an agitated Joan. I could still hear her cussing through the thin wood of the door. *That's my girl.*

"Surely you can come up with something to help protect Joan." There was no way the angels of light couldn't do something.

Gabriel exchanged looks with Sky. "Well, there is something, but I doubt if she will do it if we can't protect you too."

Sky took a step closer, his blue eyes as intense as I had ever seen them.

"I'll do anything, just tell me."

"Gabriel can place her under the protection of angelic wards," Sky explained, glancing at Gabriel. "It won't last forever, but it would buy us time to come up with a more permanent solution."

My heart leapt for joy. "That's great. Let's do it, then."

Sky raised a hand to stop me from running to Joan with the good news. "It's not that simple, Nix. She has to agree to go to a designated place, where she will have to stay until we figure things out. She won't do it unless we let you go with her."

"And I can't...." I didn't want to face Asmodeus, but I was willing to do it if it'd protect Joan. I had to come up with a way to get her to accept the plan. "Find her a place and leave the rest to me.

I will get her there." I was not sure exactly how I was going to do that, but I'd come up with something. "You're sure my master won't be able to find her, right?"

Gabriel nodded. "Yes, she will be invisible to him as long as she stays inside the wards." He looked at Sky. "Sky thought of a small abandoned cottage by the bay. We will clean it up and make it comfortable for her."

"Won't she be lonely?" I hated to think of vibrant Joan cursed to an existence of lonely days and even lonelier nights.

"Anyone can visit her. As long as she stays within the boundaries of the wards, your master will be able to see everybody but her."

Sky seemed as excited about this plan as I was sure Joan would be. Her coffee shop was scheduled to open soon, and she wouldn't be happy when she found out she would have to postpone it. "How are you going to get her there? And can't we set the wards at her place instead?"

"Asmodeus already had a sniff of this place," Gabriel said with a sneer. "He'll know there are wards right away and realize we're protecting her. In a place he has never been to, he won't be able to tell the difference."

It made a warped kind of sense. A plan was beginning to form in my head. It wouldn't end well for me, but as long as she was safe, I'd be all right. This was one of the few occasions when it stunk to be immortal. I'd much rather die than be at the mercy of my master for eternity.

We discussed some of the details, including what to do about her business. I figured we could probably trust her best friend, Tess, to keep the store's setup going, but we would have to come up with some kind of plausible reason for Joan's absence. Telling her there was a dark angel after Joan was not an option.

With nothing else to say, I walked over to Joan's bedroom and knocked. "Jo, can we talk?"

After a few moments of silence, the door creaked open and Caleb appeared, a worried glaze in his eyes. "She's inside," he said unnecessarily, opening the door wider and letting me in. "You better be worthy of her." I knew I wasn't, a dark angel with a stained soul who was hopelessly in love with her.

He exited the room and closed the door, leaving me alone with his sister. She was sitting on her bed, her face a mess of emotions— anger and confusion, maybe some fear. She should be afraid. Asmodeus was not to be taken lightly. I approached slowly, trying to gauge her mood. Joan lifted her eyes to me, and I shivered. She was mad at me. Furious.

"You are not sacrificing yourself for me, you hear?" Her voice caught as she wiped her eyes. Had she been crying?

I sat next to her, tentatively seeking her hand between us. She didn't recoil, so I covered it with mine and allowed myself a moment to breathe in her scent, all vanilla and lemon on a summer day.

"That's not what I came here to say," I started, bracing myself to lie. You would think a dark angel would be used to lying, but I couldn't remember a single instance when I had lied to anyone, mortal or angelic. I had to lie to Joan, however, if I wanted to assure her safety. "I have a proposition, Jo."

Her face brightened, a shadow of a smile lifting the corners of her lips. "It's a bit early in our relationship to think of getting married, Nix, don't you think?"

It still confused me when Joan said those kinds of things, but I was slowly beginning to understand they were meant as a joke. I smiled, happy she was feeling well enough for what she called "just messing around."

"No, not marriage." Would I even be able to marry a human? Sky was an angel, and yet he was about to get married to Caleb, with the obvious blessing of the archangel. I doubted that Asmodeus would ever agree to such a thing. Surprisingly, the idea caused me a certain sadness. "Gabriel told me that if we hide in a place unfamiliar to Asmodeus, we can avoid detection."

Joan's eyes rounded into small saucers. "That easy? We just hide somewhere else?"

I chuckled nervously. "Well, no. Gabriel will have to set up some wards around the house," I explained. "It will make you invisible to my master."

She squinted and tilted her head. "And you?"

This was the part where I had to blatantly lie to the one person I didn't want to. "Me too." Two tiny words that left acid on my tongue. *It's for her own good. For her safety.* It didn't matter what I told myself. It was a lie. I was lying to the woman I loved. I was indeed a dark angel.

Her back straightened. "Really? Me and you together?"

I lowered my head in shame, and so she couldn't read it in my eyes. "Sky found a place. We can move in a couple days."

I told her that we could talk to Tess and ask her to mind the bakery until we could come back. Then I waited, wondering, would she take the bait?

✢

## JOAN

From the window, I watched my brother and his angelic fiancé walking from the car, hand in hand. Before they reached the door, Caleb pulled Sky to him for a kiss, lips lingering, tenderly connected for a moment. I sighed. Their love for each other was both inspiring and depressing. Or at least it used to be. I had never expected to find someone I loved as much as Caleb loved his angel. Now that I had, my heart refused to face the facts—Phoenix was under the command of the darkest of angels, and he would never be mine. Not really.

"The place is ready," Caleb announced as soon as he opened the front door. Sky and Caleb had been cleaning the small cabin where Phoenix and I would hide. "We made it all cozy and pretty for my favorite sister."

I laughed and knotted my hands behind his neck in a hug. My brother was as tall as I was short, so my legs dangled until he set me down. "Thank you, guys. I will pay you in cookies when I open my store."

Sky's eyes opened wide. He loved my cookies almost as much as

Gabriel did. "Can't wait. Can you make those with the funny name?" Snickerdoodles, his favorite. I smiled and nodded. Sometimes, Sky seemed very young. He pointed at Phoenix and me. "The two of you can move in tomorrow. Pack your things, girl. Time for a vacation."

It was no vacation. Not if we were hiding from an angel of hell. But I was looking forward to being alone and rather stuck in a cabin with the angel who made me twinkle from the inside out. I hadn't been able to sleep since this whole thing was planned a couple days ago, thinking of the things we would be doing while locked in our hideout.

We had dinner together that night, squeezing ourselves around the tiny bistro table I had in my kitchen. My knee rubbed against Phoenix's, so I wrapped my leg around his, making him choke on the forkful of lasagna he'd swallowed. Caleb gave me the "behave, girl" look, but Sky only blinked, utterly confused.

After dinner, they helped me pack some items from the kitchen and stuff an icebox with food.

"Why in heaven's name would you need this many chocolate chips?" Caleb asked, staring at me with three large bags of the baking chips in his hands.

It was my turn to blush. Chocolate chip cookies were Phoenix's favorite treat, and I was planning to bake a lot of them. Sky had once told me that angels could eat as much as they wanted and never put on an extra ounce in weight. I fully intended to feed my man his favorite treats—which I was hoping included me.

In my rush to get things ready, I hadn't stopped to think why my brother, usually so protective and unreasonably fatherlike, hadn't raised a stink about the fact that his baby sister was going to be locked in a small house with the beautiful angel who loved her. Maybe he figured that if the choice was between me being kissed to an inch of my life or dying at the hands of a monster, the first option was a much better one. Even if I had all intentions of doing a lot more than kissing.

I insisted that Caleb and Sky would sleep in my room. "I will sleep on the couch," I lied. Not that they believed me, but I had to keep a sense of decorum in front of my brother. Phoenix, always a bit bewildered by our human ways, offered his bed to me instead of the couch, and Caleb almost choked on his own spit. Before he jumped and punched Phoenix out of misguided brotherly love, I ran to the rescue. "Sure, Nix. You take the couch, and I will take your bed. Get your mind out of the gutter, bro."

After Caleb and Sky had gone to bed, I lingered on the couch, my legs curled under me, my head resting on Phoenix's shoulder. We didn't say anything for a while, staring at the blank screen of the TV and listening to the beat of our own hearts. It was intimate. It was wonderful.

"I'm so happy you did the sensible thing, Nix," I finally said. "Not delivering yourself into the hands of your master, I mean."

He was quiet for a moment. "Me too." The quiet words left his lips right before he kissed me, and for a fraction of a second, I wondered whether he was trying to shut me up. I didn't care. I loved the softness of his lips and the gentle stroke of his tongue against mine.

Before I realized what I was doing, I had my hands under his T-shirt, tracing the ridges of his muscles. "Let's go to your room," I whispered, already lost in the feeling and taste of him.

"But I thought I was sleeping on the couch."

If I weren't so turned on, I would have laughed. My sweet dark angel and his penchant for literal meanings. "We can both sleep there." I moaned into his mouth, coaxing him up from the couch. "After we make love, Nix."

"Oh…." He paused for a second while I squeezed one hand between the waist of his pants and the hardness of his hips. "I like that idea."

Not any more than I did.

We stumbled together all the way to his bed, discarding items of clothing as we moved and being careful to lock the door behind us. I backed up to the edge of the bed and lay on my back, naked and wanton. Phoenix studied me from beneath his dark lashes, his desire blatantly growing as he stood there, exquisite and gloriously bare of any clothing.

When I began worrying he was not going to make a move, he climbed on the bed and crawled until he was kneeling beside me. He covered my breast with his hand, his fingers teasing my nipple into a hard bud of yearning. I moaned and writhed against his hand. He followed it with his lips, soft, warm, and thrilling over my sensitive skin. This angel learned fast.

While his lips were busy sharing the love between my breasts, his hand continued its track down my belly to caress my equally sensitive folds. I thrust my hips upward to meet his exploring fingers, but he suddenly abandoned my breast. I was disappointed until I realized he had other plans for his lips. Where his fingers had been seconds before, his mouth followed. Ecstasy, pure ecstasy. I squirmed as he settled between my legs to taste me more fully. A wave of intense pleasure and pressure began building up where his tongue performed what had to be magic, which soon spread throughout the rest of my body, an out-of-control tundra fire fanned by his breath. A loud moan escaped my lips, and I had the fleeting clarity to worry whether my brother had heard it next door. It only lasted a fraction of a second. Nix's touch was intoxicating. I felt I was going to explode at any minute, and I wanted to be connected to him when that happened. I wanted him to spiral into bliss along with me, two as one on a trip to the stars.

Phoenix seemed confused when I pulled him away from me. "Did I do it wrong?" I almost laughed. Wrong? Fuck no. I could die happily with his lips between my legs.

I flipped him over on the bed and hovered over him. A quick peek told me he was totally ready for me, and my fire spiked. If I didn't act quickly, I would climax before we were joined. "Nix, nothing you do to me is wrong," I whispered, swinging one leg over him so I was straddling his hips, his arousal touching mine. I moaned again.

This time, Phoenix didn't wait for my cue. He put his hands around my waist, pulled me up in the air as if I weighed no more than one of his feathers, and then in maddeningly slow motion, he lowered me onto him, my muscles closing around him, welcoming him. For a moment the tension eased, but when he pulled slightly out only to bury himself deeper inside me, I couldn't hold it in any longer. All the boiling pressure collected in me threatened to erupt. I think I yelled and rocked myself harder on top of Phoenix. He grunted softly and jutted his hips out to meet me before he scooted farther up the bed until his back was leaning against the headboard, his upper body now touching mine and my legs wrapped around his waist. He caressed my breast with one hand while the other flattened against my bottom, pulling me closer.

"Holy shit! I love you, Nix." The truth came out at the same time as all my muscles gave in to the building pressure, flooding my whole being in a wave of such intense pleasure, I was sure I saw heaven. I collapsed on him, my forehead against his, our breaths mingling as we came down slowly from our high. I felt him shudder underneath me and knew he had reached his release also.

He was the quietest lover I'd ever had. Not that I'd had that many—many boyfriends, but only two, maybe three lovers if you counted an embarrassing botched attempt at sex a few years before.

We didn't move for a while, enjoying our connection and the matching of our heartbeats. I sought his lips with mine and kissed him, slowly and fully, still wanting more of his heavenly flavor. The hardness beneath me surprised me at first. *He's an angel, fool.* It seemed there were quite a few other advantages to dating an angel that my brother had never mentioned to me. Not that he would ever talk to me about sex.

"You want to go again so soon?" I asked when he slipped back inside me. "I may need to rest a bit." I giggled, my lips skirting his earlobe. "But I am impressed."

Phoenix raised his face and looked me in the eye, his hazel eyes piercing deeply into my heart and soul. "Did you mean it?"

I knitted my brow, confused. "Mean what? That I'm tired?"

He shook his head and wiggled a bit so we'd fit better. With a moan, my resolve to rest before going on another love round cracked under the pressure of Phoenix swelling inside me. "Did you mean what you said? That you love me?"

Shit. I had spewed that out, hadn't I? Did I mean it? Yes, I think I did. Did I want to express it this early in our relationship? No. But Phoenix was not a regular date who may vanish into obscurity after he tired of me. Phoenix was an angel who could vanish forever, even if not of his own volition.

"Yes, I did—I do. I love you, Nix." I fixed my gaze on his, trying to read his thoughts. His serious face broke into an open smile as he hardened further, filling me completely. "Shit. Can all angels do this?"

It was his turn to be confused. "Do what?" He moved under me, sheathing himself even deeper. I let out a squeal of delight and he laughed. The bastard! He knew exactly what I was talking about. Had Phoenix really made a joke for the first time?

# CHAPTER 9
## ASMODEUS

## NIX

Sky hadn't lied when he told me the place was small and basic. I didn't know much about human houses, but I would guess this one barely qualified as such. It was made of wood and consisted of one room, a tiny bathroom, and a galley kitchen that made my girl's baker nose wrinkle in disdain. The little home was perched on a slope on a tiny island on the bay, looking as if it were getting ready to jump off and swim back to shore. It had a lovely view of the water, quiet and serene, the exact opposite of what our situation was.

Joan was exploring the island with Caleb, and Sky had stayed behind to keep me company. She had no idea what I was about to do. As Gabriel had explained to me, he wouldn't be able to protect me with the same wards he would be using on Joan. Something to do with seraphic law and the crimes of my past; he wouldn't elaborate, and I had a feeling I was better off not knowing, so I didn't press him. Joan thought Gabriel was going to shield both of us, the only reason why she'd accepted the plan. My heart, cold and unfeeling for so long, was equally bursting at the seams with love for this tiny human and hurting—lying to her was physically painful.

"Are you sure you want to do this?" Sky asked, stealing a glance at the distant figures of Joan and his fiancé. "We won't be able to do anything about it."

I swallowed the knot that had been growing in my throat. "I'm sure. I must keep Joan safe from my master." I shivered, fully aware of what would happen if Asmodeus got his hands on Joan.

"He will rip you to shreds," Sky said, his voice too soft for the others to hear.

I knew that. I had been preparing myself physically and mentally to endure the wrath of a master who was cruel even on his best days. It was not dying that I was afraid of—I was immortal, and killing another angel was not only nearly impossible but also a crime even the dark lords were not willing to commit. But I was terrified of every other way Asmodeus could make me suffer for my failure.

"I want to keep her safe, and this is the only way I know how." Love had made me stupid, but I couldn't help it.

"We could wait a bit. Maybe Gabriel can come up with something else," Sky suggested.

"You know he won't. He's forbidden to help me by rules of the Council, and Joan would refuse to do anything that would put me at risk." It made my heart swell to know that, to feel this loved when I was obviously not worthy. I would do the right thing by her. "I made my choice."

Sky sighed, rubbing a hand over his face. "Joan will kill me when she finds out I knew about this and still let you do it." She probably would, but better to be angry than dead.

Caleb and Joan joined us shortly after. I couldn't help but stare at my girl's face, her cheeks and nose tickled pink by the cold ocean wind but a warm smile on her lips.

Sky reached for Caleb's hand. "We better leave these lovebirds alone," he said, winking at Joan. His playful smile didn't reach his eyes. He was as uncomfortable with lying as I was. "We're meeting with Tess to go over some things." Joan's friend would be in charge of keeping the work going at the bakery so it could still open on schedule.

"Tell her the tile people are coming Monday and that they better have the right tile," Joan said, her voice as authoritative as always. "They were trying to sell me this crappy red tile. Tess knows which one I picked. I hope she doesn't let them bully her."

Caleb chuckled. "You must be kidding. Tess doesn't get bullied. If there is any bullying to be done, she'll be the one dishing it out."

We all said our goodbyes, and they left. Joan and I stayed by the door, watching them hop on the small boat and sail away over the light waves of the bay. There was another boat on the beach if we needed to leave the island before they came to get us, but I wouldn't be needing it. Once Asmodeus knew I was there, he'd be on me before I could finish the summons. The plan was to call my master and tell him I had lost track of the mortal girl. The tricky part was to do it while Joan was asleep so she couldn't react until both the dark lord and I were far away from her. My stomach hurt, and it wasn't because I was hungry.

"Let's go inside. It's cold out here." Joan held my hand and pulled me to the door. "How do hot chocolate and cookies sound? After we light that fire."

She had lit my fire a while back, a fire that kept me as warm as it chilled me to the bone. If I lived my life of misery before without any hope, how would it feel to go back to such an empty life now that I knew how it felt to love and be loved?

Joan struggled with the fire for a while. I couldn't help since I had no idea how to light a real fire. "Don't you angels have superpowers? Can't you just light it with a laser look?" I shook my head, confused. "What the fuck is so great about being an angel, then?" I knew she was joking around. By now I recognized her tells—a tiny smile in the corner of her lips, a twinkle in her eyes, an almost invisible dimpling of her cheek.

"I can make myself invisible from humans, travel at great speeds, fly, but not much more," I confessed, feeling weak and pitiful. "I think it has something to do with the fact that I am a fallen angel. I'm sure Sky has more skills than I do."

In a smooth move, she turned from her crouch by the fireplace and wrapped her arms around my neck. "You have amazing skills, you beautiful angel, you." She planted a kiss on my lips, and I immediately felt stronger. "The things you make me feel are better than any hocus-pocus other angels can come up with. I love you, my sweet dark angel."

I swear she could turn me into liquid with a word or a touch. For the next few hours, I forgot about my plan, forgot I was an angel, forgot I could never be who Joan thought I was, and instead I loved her with all the passion and strength of my dark soul. If I had to leave her, I wanted to go enveloped in her flames. I wanted to engrave the memory of her kisses, her hands on my body, her loving words into my brain and never let go. Those memories would see me through the bad times ahead.

Later we sat by the fire, wrapped in a blanket, sipping hot chocolate and looking at one of the books she brought with her. It was an art book. Pages and pages of beautiful pictures of artwork from around the world. About halfway through the book, she stopped on a page with a picture of a young woman, reading a letter by a window. The light that came through the glass illuminated only her face, as if the artist was telling us, "Look at her. Look at her expression, what she's thinking and feeling." Nothing else mattered. Not the heavy curtains folded over the open window, not the fruit in the discarded bowl, not the intricate red tablecloth that decorated the foreground. Interpreting her feelings was what the painting was about.

"What do you think she's reading?" Joan asked, peering closer at the picture. "She doesn't look too happy."

"She's reading the letter her lover left her before he killed himself." Now where had that come from? Why would I think that? Why not something simpler, like her parents wouldn't come to visit after all, or her lover was detained abroad?

Joan stared at me. "What? Why would you say that? A bit specific, isn't it?"

I agreed. Too specific to have come out of nowhere. Was this a memory trying to break through the fog of my mind? Something I'd seen or heard before my memories were erased? What exactly had the council erased from my mind? I couldn't tell for sure, but from the latest glimpses into what I thought were lost memories, I knew there was love, pain, and loss in my past. What could I have done to deserve an exile in hell?

## JOAN

There was a serene beauty to the dark angel sleeping next to me, his face free from all the horrors and worries that he always carried around, his full lips relaxed into a semi-smile. His dark, thick eyelashes fanned against the tan of his skin mere inches away from me. I couldn't sleep, curled on the floor by the fireplace, facing the heavenly creature who had turned my life upside down. Not that I minded; in fact, I loved him for it. Even my teenage crushes never gave me the warm, fuzzy feelings I had always associated with love. Phoenix's flames fanned the spark within me into a full-blown fire.

My mind was full of questions. What had he done to be punished so harshly? Sky once told me he had heard only terrible crimes were punished with exile to the Fortress. He himself had once feared he'd be condemned to a life as a dark angel when he broke one of the most sacred directives of angelic life—allowing my brother to live instead of harvesting his soul.

Morning was peeking through the slats of the window shutters, the random rays creating a spotlight over Phoenix. I couldn't believe he had done anything terrible. He had too good of a heart. I refused to believe that the goodness in him had sprouted from all the bad things that had happened to him. I was certain he had always been good.

A sound startled me from my musings. At first, I thought it was the motor of a boat, but then I noticed the rhythmic booms that could only come from wings—the giant wings of an angel. I jumped to my feet and went to peek through the gaps in the shutters. Outside, a magnificent angel had landed, his black wings still flapping even as his bare feet touched the sandy ground. In the weak morning light, I could see he was an exquisite male, perfect from his dark hair to his toes. He wore nothing but a loincloth, and every inch of his body was lean, well-sculpted muscle. But that perfection didn't reach his heart, because his lips were curled into a grimace and his dark eyes seemed to emit a malevolence that made me shake inside.

Asmodeus. How had he found us? We were supposed to be invisible to him.

"Minion, come forth. I know you're here." His voice scratched my ears, low and threatening. "Come out and tell me where the mortal girl is. Now!"

Before I could do anything, I heard the front door open. "Don't go outside," I yelled. But it was too late. My beautiful angel was already out, facing the monster who had tortured him for so long.

I yelled his name again, but neither he nor the evil angel seemed to hear me. Phoenix had unfurled his gorgeous wings, but even then he looked small and vulnerable, exposed to the vicious glare of his master. He fell to his knees before Asmodeus and lowered his head, his fingertips touching the cold sand beneath him.

"Angel, what have you done with the human?" The darkest angel stood erect, a tower looming over the hunched figure of my Phoenix. "I went to the house, but she wasn't there."

"Master, she has eluded me." I barely recognized Phoenix's voice, submissive and shaky. "She has vanished."

"Liar." Asmodeus lifted his hand and snapped it down over my love, an invisible whip slashing across Phoenix's skin. Blood poured from the open wounds on his shoulder and cheek. Phoenix bent over farther, making no sound even though he had to be in pain.

"She's friends with an angel," Phoenix said, his voice muffled. "He must have warned her of your coming."

Another lash of the hand and more blood sputtered up in the air. I closed my eyes; I swear I felt the sting of the invisible whip. "How would they know I was coming unless you told them?"

There was silence for a moment, and my heart accelerated in dread of what I knew Phoenix was about to do. "You're right, Master," he said finally, confirming my fears. "I told them. I won't let you take Joan."

The scream I heard must have come from me, but I couldn't tell. My focus was on what was happening outside. Asmodeus's face contorted in terrible anger, and he raised his hand higher. He would kill Phoenix. As his hand began making its way downward, I ran out of the house, screaming, "No, I'm here. Take me. I'm here."

At first nothing happened. Asmodeus cocked his head to the side as if he could hear something but wasn't sure where it was coming from. Phoenix stole a furtive glance in my direction, his eyes screaming a warning I could see but couldn't heed. The evil angel couldn't see me. Whatever angelic hocus-pocus Gabriel had done, it held steady. Even with me screaming at the top of my lungs, the angel couldn't see me. The question was, could I touch him?

Not waiting to weigh the wisdom of such a decision, I grabbed a shovel that was leaning against the side of the house and ran to Asmodeus. As I approached, I raised the garden tool higher and glanced at Phoenix, whose eyes were wide open, one of them covered in blood running from his forehead. The sight of my bleeding angel fanned my anger further. With a last burst of angry energy, I swung the shovel toward Asmodeus's head and hit it hard enough to make him stumble backward a few steps.

Phoenix jumped to his feet and ran to me. "Why did you do that? Now he can see you."

The hellish angel, not a hair displaced on his head, advanced toward me with such an irate glare in his eyes, I felt myself tremble from head to toe. My angel placed himself between me and

Asmodeus, his dark wings providing a barrier of sorts.

"Get out of the way, minion." I couldn't see Asmodeus from where I was, but I could definitely hear his low, seething voice.

"No. Take me instead, Master." Phoenix's feathers quivered as I touched them, trying to wipe the drops of blood that had lodged between them. "She's no threat to you, I promise."

A terrifying laugh echoed around us. "You stupid vermin of an angel. I don't care if she is a threat or not. I want her, and you better get out of the way."

There was no time to react. In one breath, I had been tied with something invisible but stronger than rope, thrown over Asmodeus's shoulder, and carried up into the clouds. In a panic, I searched for Phoenix and saw him being dragged behind us, his body and wings curled into an undefined mass that told me he was unconscious. Lost for a solution to the situation we were in, I did what any self-respecting woman would do when in danger—I screamed Sky's name from the top of my lungs.

"Shut up, human." Asmodeus's voice gave me the creeps as it vibrated in my ears. He didn't know me well, apparently. I upped the volume of my screaming. "Shut the fuck up!"

That was the last thing I heard him say. A blast of something both dark and bright exploded inside my head, and the world fell into complete darkness.

# NIX

A sliver of light found its way between my lashes. Try as I might, I couldn't open my eyes, eyelids as heavy as lead staying stubbornly down. I focused on my other senses instead. There was a soft rhythmic sound coming from across whatever space I was in. Not Asmodeus. The dark lord didn't do anything softly.

"Jo, is that you?" It had to be my girl. Before Asmodeus knocked me out with his seraphic blast, I had seen her awkwardly slumped over his shoulder, screaming bloody murder. Despite the direness of the situation, a smile crawled to my lips. Joan was a spitfire of a girl, and I knew that even Asmodeus wouldn't tamp her down.

When there was no answer, I felt the area around me. I was not tied anymore, so I reached for the ground beneath me. It was hard, but my fingers touched something viscous. We were at the Fortress. The walls and floors of the Fortress were made of seraphic material that absorbed the wickedness of everything within its walls and turned it into a black, gooey material that was as solid as it was porous. You could walk and lean on it, but you could also walk through it with hardly any resistance. Asmodeus and the other higher angels had the power to turn it into a solid wall if they wanted to keep others out. My master's torture chamber was one such room. The other was the storage space where the plucked souls were kept. From that room there was no escape. I avoided it at all costs. Even though I normally had to process the souls I plucked, I had developed a system that allowed me to go in and out of the holding chamber in a wink of an eye. The capsules where the souls were kept for eternity were see-through, and the images of the tortured souls within were too much for me to handle.

I blinked my eyes half open. I could see a smallish room with no furnishings, like most spaces in the Fortress, and slumped against the opposite wall was my shining star. "Jo, are you awake? Jo?" I didn't want to alarm my master, so I kept my voice low at first, but frustrated and worried by her lack of movement, I risked a louder call. "Jo, say something, please."

Joan moaned, and I dragged myself on shaky legs to where she was. Whatever Asmodeus had used to contain me on the way to the Fortress had severely impaired my muscles. My legs were soft as jelly, my arms numb and heavy. I touched Joan's shoulder as soon as I was close enough and was encouraged when she stirred against my hand.

I sat with my back supported by the wall and pulled her head onto my lap. If I felt incapacitated, I could only imagine how Joan felt as a mortal. We weren't going anywhere any time soon, so I waited, brushing my hand on Joan's beautiful face and dark hair, hoping she would wake up before Asmodeus made an appearance.

"Am I still alive?" Joan's voice snapped me from the semi-sleep I had fallen into. My brain was still fuzzy, and it took me a minute to find my bearings. I looked down at Joan, who was staring up at me with a frown. "Did I die?"

I chuckled softly and caressed her cheek with my thumb. "No, you're alive. Bent out of shape but alive."

Joan smiled and sat up, moaning. "Holy shit. I have a drum inside my head." She held on to her temples. "What the hell did that idiot do to me?"

I shook my head. "I'm not sure. Probably seraphic rope." She stared at me, narrowing her eyes. "It's hard to explain. Like an invisible rope made out of spiritual energy. It does more than hold you; it strengthens as it absorbs your energy, weakening you as it gets stronger."

"Wicked." Was it me or did Joan look almost impressed? "What about you? You don't look good."

"He knocked me out with something else, not sure what." Asmodeus was always coming up with new and improved "toys." Whatever he had used on me, it had sucked all my energy and strength. I wasn't sure I could stand, much less walk. How was I going to protect Joan in this weakened state? "Why did you have to reveal yourself, Jo?"

Joan actually snorted. "Are you kidding me? What kind of person would I be if I allowed that freak to take my boyfriend without a fight?"

Boyfriend? She thought of me as her boyfriend? Not that it mattered now that we were both pretty doomed to pain and sorrow, but my heart still swelled inside me. "An alive and healthy one," I said, unable to control the tiny smile that crept to my lips. "Boyfriend?"

When she blushed, my heart leapt for joy. Joan was not the type of girl to blush often. "Idiot," she exclaimed, the pink tint spreading over her cheeks belying the tone of voice. "Of course you're my boyfriend. We slept together, didn't we?"

"Haven't you had sex with other men before?" I had assumed she had, but my dearth of knowledge of human ways meant I was often wrong.

"Yes, I have, but what we have goes deeper." It was a mere whisper. Her face was now burning scarlet. "At least I thought it did. Was I wrong?"

I pulled her against me. "No, you're right," I hurried to say. "But I was not sure you felt the same."

With her head on my shoulder, she slapped my chest playfully. "You're a moron, Nix. Of course I feel the same. I did things with you I've never done before. I'm not the wild girl everybody thinks I am, you know."

I had never thought of her as wild but rather perfect in every way. Maybe she was not what humans considered a beauty, and she did have what her brother called a potty mouth, but she was absolutely perfect in my eyes.

"Don't you think it's weird that we're having this conversation now, knowing all too well that monster out there is going to make us hurt?" She was right. We should've been making plans to escape, not talking about our feelings. If we were going to suffer, however, we might as well let it all out while we could.

I didn't have the chance to respond. A door opened on the opposite wall, dripping with the black tar-like material, and Asmodeus stepped in. With his jet-black wings unfurled and stretched to their full height, my master was a formidable sight. Unfortunately, the crooked smile on his lips and the evil glint in his eyes turned what could be beauty into a threatening, moving mass of angelic flesh.

Our time was up.

†

JOAN

I had always thought of evil as an abstract idea, even subjective at times, but I changed my mind when Asmodeus walked into the room we were caged in. Evil was very much a solid, concrete thing, one that had the magnificent body of a fallen angel. He took a few steps toward us and stopped, ogling us like a wolf staring at a lame deer.

"You have given me quite a chase, human." His voice boomed, and I wondered whether he was doing it for effect, because I didn't remember his voice being impressive. "Now it's time to pay your dues."

I couldn't help it. I shivered against Phoenix, fear coursing through my veins like liquid nitrogen.

"Come, human." Did he really think I was going to obey him? I might've been scared, but I was not stupid enough to go meekly. If he was going to hurt me—and I was pretty sure he was—then I would go down fighting. "Come now!" His voice grew louder, a tinge of frustration seeping through.

I shook my head since I couldn't trust myself to articulate words through my chattering teeth. That seemed to enrage him. His smirk turned into a terrifying frown as he bent down to grab me.

"No, take me instead." Phoenix moved me aside and tried to stand up without much success. He braced himself on the wall, but even then his legs gave out under his weight. "She hasn't done anything against you, Master. I'm the one who failed. Send her back to Earth and do what you want with me."

Asmodeus momentarily lost interest in me to focus on my beautiful angel, struggling to get to his feet. With a roar of laughter, the dark lord threw his head back and growled. "I will deal with you later, minion. What makes you think you have a choice to submit to me? As to this human morsel, I can't wait to sink my teeth into her."

"The council will find out that you broke the united seraphic law by hurting a still-living human." Where was Phoenix getting the courage to stand up to his cruel master? Despite the trouble we were in, my heart swelled a bit in admiration.

Asmodeus squinted. "And how are they going to find out? Are you going to fly to tell them?" He laughed humorlessly. "Oh, wait! You can't because you're mine." The stress he put on that last word made me shake uncontrollably. "And I have no intention of leaving you in any condition to fly or even walk out of here."

Phoenix was still trying to stand, his breath labored from the effort. "I don't care what you do to me," he said in a tremulous voice. "But you will let her go."

"That's so sweet," the dark lord said, voice lowered. "You're in love with this mortal. How touching and so predictable coming from you, minion."

Both my angel and I looked up at the evil being standing before us. "What do you mean, predictable?"

Asmodeus sighed loudly. "Never mind. Something from your previous life. But I tire of this conversation and I want to play." He took another step toward me. "Come, let's have some fun, child of Eve."

As weak as he obviously was, Phoenix managed to throw himself between me and his master, much to my horror. "No, Phoenix. I'll go."

Asmodeus grabbed him by one of his wings as if he were an irritating mosquito and threw him hurtling through the air to crash against one of the walls. Phoenix didn't make a sound, but I screamed for him. "No, don't hurt him. Please."

The dark lord glanced at me, a sneer on his lips. "You're in love with him too. How very… romantic. I don't recommend it though. Loving this minion of mine can be disastrous for your health." I wasn't sure whether he was talking about the present or something from Phoenix's past. "Forgive me while I take care of him." He mock-bowed to me before turning back to Phoenix.

Finding a strength I didn't know I had, I jumped to my feet and stumbled toward Asmodeus, who had turned his back on me. He was faster and reached Phoenix before I could do anything. By the time I made it to where they were, he had Phoenix hanging by his wings as if by an invisible string. I took a swipe at his back, but my punch didn't even seem to register. He ignored me and continued pulling Phoenix away from that wall and onto a beam that seemed to be floating on its own near the adjacent wall. I tried to keep pace with him, but my legs were not working well. In horror, I watched him attach Phoenix's beautiful wings to the beam with something I couldn't see. Blood spurted from the punctured feathers and dripped slowly down to puddle beneath his dangling feet. Phoenix didn't say anything, and I hoped he was unconscious and oblivious of the pain his master was surely causing him.

"Stop hurting him, you monster," I yelled again, slapping at the dark master's wings. "What has he done to deserve this?"

Asmodeus turned his wicked eyes to me. "He broke the seraphic law and lost his charge. Worst crime a guardian angel can commit." Guardian angel? Phoenix had been a guardian angel? "Now that he's tied up, let's go back to us."

A clattering sound made us both turn around to find another angel standing by the door. "Forgive me, Master, but you're being summoned by the council."

Surprisingly, the same creature who didn't seem bothered by anything cringed a little. He paused for a moment and then turned to follow the other angel. "I'm not finished with you. This is only a reprieve."

Asmodeus left and my legs almost gave out beneath me. I looked back at Phoenix, still hanging from the floating beam, blood staining his feathers and skin. What could I do? He was too high up for me to reach him, and even if I did, I had a feeling he was being held up by some kind of angelic voodoo. How could a simple human break a spell like that?

I dropped to the floor a few feet away from Phoenix and did

something I hadn't done in a long time—I cried.

## NIX

The world revealed itself slowly and gradually to me. My eyes were open—at least I thought they were—but everything was a blur, the tar-black room dancing in waves in front of me. I couldn't feel much either, which I was sure was a blessing in disguise. Whatever Asmodeus was involved in always caused pain of some kind. I shook my head in a weak attempt at clearing it, but all I succeeded in was to further confuse my senses.

Better stand still for a moment.

Was that whimpering I heard coming from below me? Below? Where was I? Was I flying? I tried to move my wings, but I couldn't. I tried harder and an overwhelming pain shot through them into the rest of my body. Lifting my numb arms, I felt around me and found nothing but air. Not flying, then. Floating? How could I be floating while unconscious? Then it hit me—Asmodeus had me hanging somewhere. More pain would be coming soon, I knew. It wasn't the first time he had done that. The last time, he neglected to bring me down for days. The cyclic regeneration of my blood, feathers, and flesh only made it more painful. Every time the wounds closed, the seraphic nails ripped it open again.

I heard it again, a quiet sobbing wafting up to me. "Jo!" My mind cleared suddenly. Joan was there with me. Had Asmodeus hurt her? "Jo, are you all right?"

"Thank God," she said. "I'm fine. I want to bring you down, but I don't know how."

I searched for her, but she was out of my visual range. "I can't see you," I said. "Can you move elsewhere?"

The body of my heart and soul scooted into sight. I sighed, relieved. She didn't look hurt, just tired. "I'm here, Nix. Tell me what I can do."

A quick glance at the tip of my wings told me there was nothing she could do. "Nothing, unless you have angelic powers." I tried to keep my tone light, but I was not successful. I sounded scared and helpless even to my own ears.

Joan stared up at me, her eyes shining with tears. "There must be something I can do, Nix," she said before a sob stopped her. "Please, tell me there is something I can do."

I wished I could tell her there was, but my situation was pretty hopeless. So was hers, and that worried me more than the throbbing pain quickly spreading along my wings. "Check the walls. See if you can go through them." As soon as I said it, I knew how foolish that was. Even if she could escape the Fortress, what would she do? She was not an angel. She couldn't fly. "Are you hurt?"

Her voice was unusually subdued, as sobs made her hiccup after every word. "I'm fine, don't worry about me. It's you who's hurt. You're bleeding, Nix. That monster did something to your wings."

The pain was growing steadily, but I didn't want her to know that. "I'm okay. Angels don't feel pain as humans do," I lied.

"Bullshit, Nix," she exclaimed. "You forget I have an angel for a brother-in-law. I know you hurt like humans do. And bleed." A loud sob escaped her lips. "Oh, God, Nix. So much blood."

I had trained myself throughout a lifetime of pain to not react to it. No screaming, no crying out loud, no whimpering. I had mastered the art of keeping it all inside, and I was never as happy about that as now. I didn't want Joan to think I was suffering.

The only door to the room opened suddenly, and an angel I didn't recognize stepped in. "Human, you're free to go," he said. "I'll take you down to Earth."

We both looked at the messenger. "What about Phoenix?"

"Who's Phoenix?" the angel asked.

Joan pointed at me, her usual sass momentarily restored. "Hello? The angel hanging by his wings. Are you fucking blind?"

The angel threw me a perfunctory glance and dismissed me just as quickly. "He's Asmodeus's. He stays."

"No way, you fucking angelic pile of shit," Joan yelled out. "I'm not going without him. Get him down."

"Jo, please, go with him," I pleaded. "Before it's too late. Go."

Joan glanced up at me, fury mixing with fear in her beautiful brown eyes. "No, Nix. I won't leave you here to suffer at the hands of that monster. No way."

Desperate, I turned to my fellow angel. "Do something about it, angel. Take her before the master changes his mind."

"Order from the council," the angel said, his expression softening. "He won't change his mind. She's leaving."

Joan grunted. "Not without Nix. He's coming with us."

The angel glanced up at me first and then waved a hand in Joan's direction. "Sorry, human. You have no choice here." And my mortal girlfriend fell to her knees before sliding all the way to the floor.

I watched as the angel scooped her into his arms and carried her out the door, tears dancing in my eyes. "Goodbye, my love," I whispered as they disappeared behind the closing door. "Thank you for loving me, Jo."

I closed my eyes and welcomed the distraction of excruciating pain.

# CHAPTER 10
## DARKNESS

## JOAN

"You have to get out of bed, Joan." Caleb's voice came to me muffled by the pillow I had over my head. "You can't keep doing this. You're not helping yourself or Phoenix by quitting life."

I grunted but didn't move. I didn't want to go on with life. I hated that the world hadn't stopped turning on its axis, that the sun still rose in the skies every morning and the moon showed its face at night. How could things be so normal when Phoenix was in the hands of a monster suffering God only knew what atrocities? I had begged, I had cried, I had threatened, but Gabriel refused to even come to see me.

"There's nothing he can do, Joan," Sky tried to explain. "His hands are tied by seraphic law. Phoenix belongs to Asmodeus."

"What about the big boss? How can I get word to him?" I had asked, still confused about who the "big boss" really was. "He was the one who gave you special dispensation to live on Earth."

"Joan, I have no power to speak to the boss," Sky said, sitting on the edge of the bed. "I wouldn't know how to find him or how to get in touch with him."

So I vegetated in bed, barely eating or drinking, my heart crushed under the weight of knowing my boyfriend, my sweet angel, was hurting and there was nothing I could do about it.

"All right, girl. This is ridiculous." The voice was not male. The surprise made me throw the pillow aside and turn my head to see who it belonged to. Tess was standing by the bed, her arms crossed over her chest and a frown on her face. "Get your butt in gear, woman."

As usual, I obeyed. I wiped the snot off my face with the pillow, swung my legs over the edge of the bed, and stared up at my friend with what I hoped was a contrite expression on my face. "Gabriel won't even talk to me," I whined, a tight knot in my throat.

"Oh, sweetie." She didn't have to say anything else. I threw myself in her arms and burst out crying, my tears quickly soaking her T-shirt. "Let it all out, Jojo. Let it all out."

I did. I cried so hard and for so long that I couldn't feel my nose, and my eyes were so bloated I probably looked like a puffer fish. But the pressure in my chest had eased a bit, just enough so I could breathe again. And think. I needed to have my wits about me if I was ever going to find a way to save my angel from the hands of Asmodeus.

"You stink, my friend." Under Tess's close supervision and insistence, I changed my clothes and washed up a bit before emerging from my room, my hiding place for the past few days. "The situation demands some baking, don't you think?"

I giggled and followed her to the kitchen, where Caleb and Sky were brewing coffee and washing a few dishes. "Sis, so happy to see you moving again." Caleb smiled and gave me one of his bear hugs. "I have a cup of coffee here for you."

The coffee did smell heavenly, and I took a deep sniff, holding the warm cup between my hands like a buoy during a storm. "I want to talk to Gabriel, Sky."

Sky actually groaned. "Tarnation, girl. I told you already, Gabriel refuses to talk to you."

I took a large sip, the warmth of the brew sliding down my throat soothing and exciting all at the same time. "But he stepped in to rescue me. Why won't he do the same for Nix?"

"Asmodeus was breaking seraphic law by having you in his custody," Sky explained for the tenth time. "Phoenix is a dark angel in his service. He's not breaking any laws."

The same frustration and anger that had been boiling inside of me since I had been freed erupted again. I didn't want to yell at Sky. It was not his fault. I bit my lip before speaking. "Isn't it against the law to torture another angel? Weren't there laws put into effect after Samael tortured you in the Fortress?"

Caleb stepped forward and laid his hands on my shoulders. "Sis, you have to let it go. What can be done is being done, and no amount of bitching about it is going to change a thing."

"I can't accept it, Caleb. I can't. He's all alone with that monster. Do you have any idea what he does to him? What he could do?"

Caleb sighed, a deep crease on his forehead. "Have you forgotten what Samael did to Sky? Yes, I know what the dark masters can do." He drew me in for a hug. "Joan, I know it's hard to know someone you love is suffering, but you have to try and be patient and trust that the council and Gabriel are doing all they can to help him. In the meantime, you must go on with your life, be the strong woman you always are, and be here for him."

Phoenix would have agreed with him, I knew. I could almost hear him say, "I'd never forgive myself if I was the reason for you giving up on life."

"I'll tell you what you're going to do, Jojo," Tess said, pulling me away from my brother's comfortable embrace. "You're going to drink that coffee, chew on something nutritious, and then we are both going to walk down to your bakery and get busy finishing it up for the grand opening next week."

An alarming thought popped into my mind. "Shit. My job. Am I fired?" I had been away for more than a week, absent without permission or justification. I was sure to lose the one job that was keeping me afloat while my bakery was still in its infancy.

Caleb shook his head. "No, I called them as soon as you went to the cabin and told them we had a family emergency. Just give them a call when you have a chance."

The cabin. All the fantasies I had designed around that tiny place and being alone with Phoenix had been so quickly crushed, I hadn't even had time to give it any thought. "How did you know we had been taken?" Another thought crossed my mind. I snapped my head in Tess's direction. "And how aren't you freaked out about this whole conversation about angels and demons?"

Tess laughed. "I should be, shouldn't I? But this is better than watching *Game of Thrones*." I glanced at Sky, who smiled sheepishly and shrugged. He was up to something. "You dating an angel, your brother marrying another. Holy fuck, Jojo, your family is a paranormal romance come to life."

Sky escorted me to my room so I could finish getting ready while the others milled around the kitchen, drinking coffee and chatting. He leaned in close and whispered, "Angelic voodoo. She'll forget all about the angels as soon as she leaves this house." I opened my mouth and stared at him. How sneaky of him. "Gabriel's orders. We don't want to put Tess in any danger."

I turned around, rose on my tiptoes, and planted a kiss on his cheek. "Thank you, Sky. I'm so glad you're in our lives."

I stood by the door to my room, watching Sky walk back to the kitchen, a silly smile plastered on his face. Yes, I was so very happy to have him in our lives. Now if I could only bring Phoenix back to me, my world would be perfect.

# NIX

Epic fail. I remembered that—I had failed at my mission to guard him. What I couldn't remember was who he was and why I was guarding him. My lost memories were beginning to resurface, one unconnected chunk after another. My mind couldn't make sense of any of it, slivers of memories coming in as separate parts of a puzzle I had to somehow put together again. These thoughts kept me sane—or as sane as I could be in my situation. They kept me from constantly praying for the oblivion of death and distracted me from the pain.

Asmodeus had moved me to his chamber of horrors right after Joan left, and I hadn't seen another sight since then. He kept me tame by clipping my wings so I couldn't fly and making sure I was incapacitated enough not to try finding my way out of the room. Not that it mattered. The walls had been sealed, and as the powerless angel that I was, even with all my strength and wits, there was no chance I'd be able to break through the wards.

I curled up in a corner of the dark room, my knees almost touching my chin, trying hard to ignore the uncomfortable pinching of the clips that secured my wings and prevented them from unfurling. Funny that I would focus on the simply annoying feeling when my body was recovering from wounds and bruises that caused much more pain. I opened my eyes for a moment and spotted a shred of the T-shirt I'd been wearing when I was captured by my dark master. For some reason, the sight of the black cotton fabric made me choke, tears burning in my eyes and a sad rage scorching my heart.

The sound of the door opening made me shake. I was not ready for another round of torture, of abuse. My heart raced in my chest and I gasped, unable to breathe properly. But it wasn't Asmodeus. A smallish angel I had never seen before approached quietly, stealing glances behind him and signaling me into silence.

"I have to be quick. Asmodeus will soon be back," he said when he came close enough that I could hear him. "Be strong. It won't be long now."

What did he mean? Was I dying? Was my wish to put an end to my immortal life of misery finally coming true?

"Gabriel is working on a plan to free you," he explained, his eyes darting all around him. "Be strong and hold on a bit longer."

Gabriel was trying to help me? Could this be true, or was it another creative way my master had found to torture me? Giving me hope only to snatch it away again.

"I have to go now, but you're not alone." The angel moved quickly out the door, closing the darkness inside with me. The pain was still there, and I knew that soon enough, Asmodeus would walk through that same door, refreshed and excited about trying some new toy on me. Yet the weight on my chest had somehow lifted enough that I could breathe, and inside me the little spark of hope was warming and filling me with the courage I needed to endure what lay ahead.

# JOAN

At the last minute, I had decided against the bright polka-dot furnishings. It just wasn't me. I was plain and natural, the down-to-earth one everybody came to when in need of some serious grounding. Not that I didn't appreciate the splash of color across the counter and the curtains on the windows, but it didn't feel right. Especially now that my boyfriend was being held by a prince of evil. My brother had attracted an angel of light, and I'd fallen in love with an angel of darkness. If that didn't say something about me, I didn't know what would.

"Where in the hell is that gorgeous man of yours? He could be helping us now."

Tess had long forgotten about Phoenix's angelic nature or anything to do with the unbelievable side of my story. Sky's juju had worked like a charm. She seemed to remember everything except the details we didn't want her to know.

"He had to go out of town for a family emergency." I hated having to lie to my best friend, but what else could I do? I couldn't put her in harm's way.

"Where do you want these?" Ally, Tess's current girlfriend, popped out from behind the counter with the black curtains in her hands. I had chosen a delicate lace that, however dark, mimicked the beauty of Phoenix's wings. "Kind of a weird color for a bakery, isn't it?"

Tess shook her head and hooked an arm around the other girl's neck. "Silly girl. If you knew my friend better, you'd know it's the perfect color scheme for her." Ally laughed and twisted out of Tess's hold. "Both windows, sweetheart."

The bakery was opening in a couple days, but all the excitement was gone. Here I was about to turn a longtime dream into reality, and all I could think of was my angel still in the hands of his diabolic master. Without him, why was I even doing this? Wouldn't it be better to postpone the opening? The part of me that was sensible and realistic told me that I needed to go on with my life, that as much as I loved Phoenix, life couldn't stop because he wasn't around. How many women before me had lost spouses and kept going? Phoenix would most likely be pissed if I gave up because of him.

We spent the whole day finishing up with little decorative touches. The lacy curtains, the black-feather prints on the furniture and the walls, the black runners on the white tiled floor, and my most precious piece of decor, a life-size set of black wings hanging on the wall behind the counter. Phoenix would approve, I knew. My heart shrank inside my chest, sadness overtaking me. Why couldn't he be here with me, sharing this momentous event in my life?

"Holy shit. Who's the hottie?" Ally squealed rather than spoke.

Tess's head popped up from underneath the wobbly table she was trying to balance. "Is it male or female?"

I threw a glance out the window, mildly curious to whom she was referring, and saw Sky approaching the store with that gliding step he had. Tess groaned. "Hey, I thought you liked girls," she protested with a frown.

Ally laughed and looked back at her. "I'm pretty flexible both ways." Her burst of laughter exploded in the semi-quiet of the store. "Are you jealous, sweetie?"

"Me, jealous? Never." But I could tell she was. Tess discarded her girlfriends as if they were disposable, but there was something different about the way she acted around Ally. Was it possible that she was finally in love?

I followed the conversation with a lot more apathy than I would normally dedicate to such an exchange between my best friend and her current love interest. Opening the front door, I met Sky outside. I wanted to make sure the girls wouldn't hear anything they shouldn't.

Despite my resolve to not get excited or too hopeful, my heart was racing as I threw my arms around Sky's neck. "Please tell me you have good news."

Sky darted his eyes toward the store. My back was turned to the building, but I would bet both Tess and Ally were snooping from one of the windows. "Not much, I'm afraid. But Gabriel did say that things are progressing well."

"What the fuck does that mean?" I was beyond frustrated with this game of riddles Gabriel kept playing with me. "Progressing from and to where? Can't he stop being a dickhead and speak in plain English?"

Sky bent down and planted a kiss on my forehead. "That's how the higher angels are, Joan. I'm sure he is doing all he can, but angels live by strict rules. Look what kind of trouble I got myself into by breaking one rule to save your brother."

"Angels are fuckers—present company excluded." I crossed my arms like a small girl having a tantrum. Sky laughed and pulled me in for a hug. "I want answers, Sky. Answers, not riddles I can't make heads or tails of."

My brother's angel stopped laughing and patted my back with one hand while cradling the back of my head with the other. I allowed a few rogue tears to roll down from my eyes and be absorbed by Sky's T-shirt.

"I know, I know," he whispered, rocking me gently in his arms. For an angel of death, Sky had a weird talent to soothe my nerves. "Caleb sends his love. He is working today and couldn't get off." He pulled me away from him. "Look. Gabriel can be a dick, but if he says he's doing something, you can be sure he is. It could happen at any time, Joan. Have faith."

Ever since that day when my parents' souls were taken away by an angel of death while my brother and I were semiconscious in the back seat of the mangled car, I'd had faith. As painful as it was to lose my mom and dad at such an early age, the presence of that angel had comforted me during such a traumatic experience. So I believed. I believed in something bigger and mightier than us humans. But lately I was beginning to think that that was not necessarily a good thing.

"Caleb and I are talking about postponing our wedding," Sky said, wiping a tear from my face with his thumb.

"No way." I was not going to let this mess interfere with my brother's life, the man who'd given up on his youth to be the parent I had lost. Those two deserved all the happiness in the world, and I was not going to rain on their parade. "The wedding stays."

Sky bit his lip. "But we feel terrible planning such a happy event while you and Phoenix are suffering."

"I'll help you with the plans." It would distract me from my woes. Between setting the store up for the grand opening and helping them with the prep for their wedding, I would have less time to wallow in my own misery. "How can I help?"

A sunny smile burst onto his lips. "We could use your help picking the menu for the reception," he said. "We're having it catered from a local place."

"You guys have been out here for a long time." It was Tess, her lips twisted into a comical frown. "Are you guys having an affair? That would be brutal. Kind of sexy, but so wrong."

I hurriedly wiped the vestiges of tears from my face before turning to my uncouth friend. "You have such a fucking dirty mind. We're planning his wedding, not screwing behind my brother's back." I winked at Sky, who always seemed confused when Tess made one of her dirty jokes. "We're planning to go check out the food for the reception."

Tess's eyes lit up. "Ooh, food. Can I go too?"

I laughed and looked at Sky for a reaction. He nodded, a tiny smile lifting one corner of his lips. "Sure. What the hell. If there is one thing you're good at, it's eating." And apparently distracting me from the worst of my problems.

## NIX

Darkness had swelled over me until it covered my world completely again. My heart had all but stopped beating, since my angel heart needed hope and light to keep pumping blood through my body. I was nearly dead. Not as in not existing anymore—my physical body would go on probably until eternity—but my soul was shriveling to a charred chunk of spiritual coal. Somewhere in the far recesses of my mind, the memory of my love for Joan still shed some light into my otherwise bleak existence.

My days—or nights, I couldn't tell—came and went the same way. I was not allowed to pluck souls any longer; Asmodeus kept me in his chamber, sometimes chained to the wall, sometimes loose, but always captive and made to submit. The angel who had come to tell me Gabriel was working toward my release never came back, and since then the door only opened to my cruel master. So when the door opened that day, I didn't even bother to look. It was easier with my eyes closed, or maybe it was too terrifying for me to see what was coming.

"Angel, get up." It took me a few seconds to realize that was not my lord's voice. I opened my eyes then, half-blinded by the light the visitor had brought in with him. Gabriel was standing before me, his tall frame towering over me. I peeled my body from the floor to sit up and stare at the archangel. "You need to get up. You're coming with me."

A small quake stirred inside my heart. Was it possible? Were they releasing me from my master? "Where are you taking me?" My throat ached, unused to speech.

"You will stand trial before the council again," Gabriel said, extending a hand to help me up. "Asmodeus broke several seraphic laws by torturing you. We needed proof before we could take you away from his grip."

My legs were weak and wobbly under my weight, and I had to brace myself against the wall not to fall. "But then why do I have to stand trial?" What crime was I being accused of exactly?

"It's a retrial of sorts. We can release you from Asmodeus, but we have to figure out what to do with you after that," Gabriel explained, handing me a pair of pants. "Put these on. I'm taking you to see Joan."

My heart almost jumped out of my chest. Joan. I was going to see my love, my reason for living. "Really?" I wasted no time slipping into the pair of jeans. My shaking hands made it difficult, and I dropped them several times.

Gabriel frowned. "Don't get too excited," he said. "Because I owe Sky a favor or two, I am allowing you a visit to say goodbye."

What did he mean? "Goodbye? Why?"

"You won't be allowed to go back to Earth after the trial," Gabriel said, his eyes not quite meeting mine. "After all, you are still paying your dues for your crime."

Maybe the pain and the isolation of the past few days—maybe weeks, I really had no idea—had made me lose my wits, because

I cried in frustration, "The crime I don't even remember or know what it was?"

Gabriel sighed, his face showing genuine concern for the first time. "Angel, I can't tell you what it was. That's part of your punishment. I hope one day you'll remember, but I won't be the one telling you. Let's go."

Still numb, I followed the archangel out of the hated room and into the hallways of the Fortress. Several other dark angels watched our progress with faint curiosity until we crossed the porous walls of the compound. Outside it was hot and humid as usual, the reddish tint of the clouds reminding me of the famous painting by Edvard Munch. What was it called? *The Scream,* one of the most iconic paintings in the world—but how did I know this? Why did I keep having these flashes about art?

Gabriel unclipped my wings and helped me unfurl them one dark feather at a time. They had been bound for too long, and movement was painful and slow, but they eventually spread to their widest span. It felt wonderful to be able to stretch my wings and my arms, standing on my own two feet, feeling the outside air, even if it was hot and uncomfortable.

"How long do I have?" I asked, following him to the edge of the cloud where the Fortress was built. I had heard it called Hell's End often enough that the name stuck in my head. I was not too sure this was the end of my particular hell, but a good step at least.

Gabriel turned to me, raising his eyebrows. "What do you mean?"

"To say goodbye to Joan." The words left my mouth and lodged themselves in my chest, a dull throbbing pain that only grew when my thoughts wandered to my girlfriend. "How long am I allowed with her?"

"Not long, angel, not long," he said, shaking his head. "A day or two. I had to ruffle a lot of feathers to get you this, angel."

I stopped and looked up at him. "My name is Phoenix, Archangel." I didn't want to be referred to as the anonymous dark angel who nobody knew and nobody cared about. I had someone who loved me now. I wasn't a nobody anymore.

"Phoenix." Gabriel tasted the name as if tasting an exotic food. Then he smiled. "Appropriate."

"What do you mean?"

Gabriel resumed his trek to the edge. "Like a phoenix, you may yet rise from the ashes."

# CHAPTER 11

## GOODBYES

## JOAN

Cross-legged on the cold tile floor of the bakery, I looked around me in a mixture of awe and sadness. The store looked amazing with its darker hues—a dream come true. But I couldn't share my happiness with the one person I wanted to the most.

*Where are you, Nix? Are you all right?*

I'd had a long day at my part-time job, going through the motions, not quite paying attention to what was going on around me. For all I knew, the building was empty—I couldn't remember talking to or seeing a single person, and yet I knew I must have. My head was in another place, a dark place I had seen only once and wished I could forget.

"It looks amazing," Tess said, dropping to the floor beside me.

She drew her legs up until her chin was resting on her jeans-covered knees. "How excited are you about the opening tomorrow?"

I shrugged. The part of me that was excited was overshadowed by the bigger part of me that couldn't stop mourning my boyfriend. Yes, I was mourning now. A couple weeks had passed, and there was no sign of any possible rescue. Knowing what Phoenix had told me about Asmodeus's wicked games, I was almost certain I had lost the angel I knew. A stubborn thread of hope still hung on for dear life, but I had been preparing for the worst.

"Come on, Jojo. Don't let a stupid boyfriend ruin your day." After Gabriel swiped her memory of all angelic activity, Tess was under the impression that Phoenix had left me. "This is your dream, friend. Enjoy it to the fullest."

I held the sob that rose in my throat. "I know, Tess. I'm just in a funk," I said. "I'll be okay tomorrow."

Tess draped an arm over me and pulled me until I had my head on her shoulder. "I'm sorry, Jojo. I can tell how much you cared for this guy." Love was more like it. "He did seem like a really good guy. Goes to show you never know about people, do you?"

We sat there for a while, quiet in a way only good friends could be together. Afterward, we locked the bakery and Tess walked me to my house, where she had left her scooter. I waved goodbye, then headed into my dark house, not bothering to turn on the lights. I wanted to curl on the couch where I had sat with Phoenix so many times and cry my eyes out.

"That won't be necessary," a voice said.

I jumped, startled. It was Gabriel. I couldn't quite see him, but his voice had become so familiar to me that I could recognize it anywhere. "Fuck, Gabriel, you about gave me a heart attack. Stop being so creepy."

I switched on the lights and my legs turned to mush. Phoenix was standing next to the archangel, dressed in a pair of old jeans I didn't recognize and a black T-shirt. He was silent with suspiciously shiny eyes. Ignoring the fact that I had lost all strength in my limbs, I ran and threw myself in his arms. He didn't hug me back.

"What's wrong? What did they do to you?" I noticed his hands hadn't moved from their spot in front of him.

"His hands are tied," Gabriel explained, even though I couldn't see any ties. "I will cut them off soon enough, but we must go over a few things first."

What the hell was he talking about? My heart was jumping for joy, and all I wanted to do was bury myself between Phoenix's arms and absorb his warmth. "What things? And why isn't Nix talking?"

"He's under a spell of sorts. He won't be able to say anything until I'm finished." It was official—angels were the cruelest creatures in this universe.

"Let him go. You were supposed to free him, not imprison him again."

"He is what you'd call a prisoner, since he is still atoning for his crime." I was so sick of hearing about this crime that no one seemed willing to tell me or Phoenix about. "We were able to free him from Asmodeus. One of the dark angels is working for us, and he confirmed that the dark lord was torturing Phoenix. Torturing a fellow angel is forbidden by law, so the council was able to negotiate his release."

I blinked, my mind reeling from confusion. "So what's the problem exactly?"

Phoenix's eyes latched on to mine, a prayer in his expression.

"The problem, young lady, is that no matter what happened, Phoenix did commit a crime, for which he has been sentenced to a lifetime of service as a lower dark angel. There's no getting away from that."

I still couldn't understand what he was saying. "What does that mean? That he will be returned to the Fortress, the same place where he has been tortured for God knows how long?"

Gabriel stole a glance at Phoenix, who was biting his lip as if he wanted to say something. "Yes, that is exactly what it means. Except we will be making sure he won't be tortured anymore."

A quick look at my angel told me Gabriel was telling the truth. "Then why did you bring him here? Can he serve his time here?"

For once, the archangel's face dropped and concern colored his expression. "No, I brought him here so you have a chance to say goodbye." My heart skipped a beat. "I will free him once you promise not to try and hide him. It would be futile anyway."

"Goodbye? Can't he pop in once in a while when he's on Earth?" Words stumbled out of me in an erratic torrent. "I won't hold him here. He'll just visit—"

Gabriel shook his head. "Sorry, Joan. This is goodbye forever.

The council won't budge on this. Do you promise?"

What else could I do? I had to promise so he would untie him and remove the muting spell. I nodded, my throat tight with choking sobs. "I promise. I promise. Let him go."

With a wave of his hand, Gabriel broke whatever was holding Phoenix's wrists together and blocking his voice. Phoenix sighed loudly, like someone who'd been holding his breath for too long. "Jo." His eyes sought mine, but he didn't have to search for long. I had already stepped closer, my eyes locked on his perfect features and my hands reaching out for his.

"Nix." It was a whisper loaded with equal parts of happiness, relief, and sadness. I was going to lose him. I buried my face in the bunched-up fabric on his chest, inhaling his intoxicating scent and wishing for everything I couldn't have. "I love you so much."

Gabriel coughed and we both looked at him, suddenly aware of his presence. "I have to go. Angel—Phoenix, you have two days. Make it count." There was an odd tone to his voice as he said those last words. Was he trying to tell us something? Could it be that all was not lost?

As soon as the tall archangel vanished, I turned to my boyfriend. "Did you hear that?"

Phoenix arched his eyebrows. "Hear what?"

I huffed a bit. "The tone of voice. Gabriel thinks there might be a way out of this." I was sure of it.

His mouth fell open and he squeezed my shoulders gently. "Can you read minds now? Because I heard no such thing."

"Between the lines, Nix, between the lines." I waved my hand in the air and bit my lip, already lost in thought. What could we possibly do to change the council's judgment? "I'm not letting you go without a fight, Nix. I have never been a quitter."

Phoenix's smile went from his lips to his eyes. "I love you, Jo. I love every bit of you inside and out, and I will follow you anywhere you wish me to." He hugged me tighter. "Where are we going?"

"Heaven bound, Nix. We are heaven bound."

## NIX

Joan's eyes glazed over when she was plotting, her lower lip caught between her teeth and her fingers tapping on her thighs. Even though angels didn't need to bathe, I felt dirty after my time with my master, so I took a long shower before finding her sitting on the edge of the bed, that plotting aura shining all around her. Maybe I should have been scared—not all of Joan's plans were good ideas—but instead I was in awe of her understated beauty and the way she made me feel even when every inch of my body still ached from Asmodeus's cruel games.

I didn't realize I had been staring at her until she giggled and said, "Hey there, sexy angel. Get over here so I can take care of that annoying towel." It took me only a couple steps to stand knee to knee with her. Her breath caught and her smile was replaced by something else; her eyes softened and her lips went slack. "I can't lose you."

"I don't want to lose you either, Jo," I admitted, my body already responding to her proximity. "Not now, not ever."

Joan released a soft moan, and in one swift move, she pulled the towel from around my waist and dropped it by our feet. I loved the way she made my body come alive as if disconnected from my brain. She pulled me down to her and kissed me, her hand wandering teasingly over my lower body. The fire she lit inside me was already roaring out of control when she raised her arms, inviting me to undress her.

"We're running out of time," she whispered as I pulled her shirt over her head and nibbled on her lower lip. "I want to feel every inch of you, taste you, and breathe you in so I can remember every detail, every nuance of you."

I brushed a hand over her breasts and then knelt between her knees, my fingers prying her jeans open and sliding them down her legs as she shifted to make it easier for me. Soon we were both naked, shaking in anticipation, our breaths mixing and mingling as our lips met again and again. I couldn't get enough of her, and the knowledge that our time together was coming to an end fueled that hunger.

I flicked my tongue over her sweet skin, from her perfect breasts, down her belly, and lower still. With another whimpering sound that made me harder, Joan wrapped her legs around me, and I shook as desire ran through me in waves of liquid heat. I pushed her gently backward onto the bed and settled between her legs, ready to taste her, but she cupped my chin and looked at me with an unfamiliar glint in her eyes.

"Come here, Nix," she said. "Come to me."

Not sure of what she meant, I slid over her, pulling her all the way on top of the bed. Our bodies were glued together, every inch of her softness touching me. I trembled, half in ecstasy, willing thoughts of the future from my mind. Before I could say anything, she swallowed me whole, lips and tongue working their magic on mine, passionate and as yielding as resistant. One minute she was the subject of my touch, the next she was the aggressor, fingers busy exploring every ridge and valley of my back until her hands cupped my buttocks. With a sudden jerk, she pressed me closer to her, her mouth whispering warm nothings in my ear. There was desperation in her moves. I didn't know much about the lives of humans, but I knew desperation intimately.

"Jo, what's wrong?" I breathed out as her lips trailed down the side of my neck. My eyes flickered closed and I moaned. Her touch was magic. I didn't want her to stop, but I could tell something was wrong.

"I don't want to lose you, Nix," she blurted out in a choked voice. "I want to go to bed with you every night and wake up in your arms every morning. I want to feel you here. And here." She punctuated her words with a caress alongside my torso, my hips, my back. "I won't let them take you away from me, ever."

Her sobbing sobered me up as fast as a cold shower. I lifted myself on one arm to look at her. Tears streaked her beautiful face, and my heart bled a little more. I slid off her until we were lying side by side, facing each other. I wiped her tears with my hand, brushing a lock of her hair away from her face. "Don't cry, Jo. I don't want to leave you either, but there are more powerful forces at play here. We have to accept it."

Joan shook her head. "No, I won't accept it." She cried harder, and I pulled her into my arms. Her tears fell onto my shoulder, red hot and painful, rolling over the birds of my tattoo.

Helplessness took me under its insidious mantle. What could I do? I knew I had failed at guarding one of my charges but couldn't remember anything else about my crime. I held her for a while, listening to her gentle sobs, tears burning behind my own eyes, my stomach soured by the injustice of it all.

We made love later, slowly, gently, almost as if we were afraid to hurt each other, and then we fell asleep in each other's arms. I woke up first, the early rays of light beginning to dilute the dark of the night. I knew her bakery café was opening today, and I didn't want to spoil it for her. Neglecting to put on clothes, I tiptoed to the kitchen and made her coffee. I wanted to spend some time with her doing what we always did, and time was running out.

When I returned with the coffee, she was up, sitting with her back against the headboard. She had put on a white T-shirt and was semi-covered by a blanket. I handed her the coffee mug with a smile and then climbed next to her, sliding my legs under the covers and cuddling against her side. "Shall we watch TV?" I asked as if nothing pivotal was about to happen to us.

Joan nodded and grabbed the TV remote from the bedside

table. We didn't care what was on, but we needed the sound of normalcy, the ordinary at that moment. Something familiar to anchor us, to give us the illusion everything was fine. The news was on. Behind the anchorman was a picture of a small painting, an abstract representation of pain in reds and purples, streaks of paint and blood-like spatters.

My eyes widened. I knew that painting.

"In an auction in New York City this weekend, a small painting from an otherwise unknown artist fetched a bid of over one million dollars from an anonymous buyer who will donate it to the Metropolitan Museum," the anchorman said. My heart beat faster as recognition hit me one pixel at a time. "Twenty-five years ago, Anthony Mello was a young artist from Toronto who never achieved much success in life. Mello is thought to have suffered from depression and was found dead one morning by the cleaning crew at the studio he worked at." Something was exploding in my chest. "The police deemed it a suicide. His life is covered in mystery. With no family and not many friends, he left behind a suicide note dedicating his life's work to the love of his life, someone he referred to simply as 'my angel.'"

"Are you okay, Nix?" Joan held on to my hand. I was shaking violently, and my breathing had turned shallow and too fast. "What's wrong?"

A memory of a young human in his twenties, pigment-stained fingers, and the loveliest smile assailed me. I remembered Anthony. I remembered everything about him—the way he woke me up every morning with a long, heated kiss; the way his hands caressed me at night; the way his body felt against mine. Anthony was my lover. No, not my lover—my love.

"Anthony and I were—" The words died in my lips. My young artist lover had taken his own life while his guardian angel was too distracted by love to notice he had given up on life.

That guardian angel had lost his charge.

That angel was me.

## JOAN

The silence was oppressive and awkward. Phoenix hadn't said anything since he'd seen the news about the auction. His olive skin had paled to a ghostly white, and even his lips had lost their normal color. His eyes were what shocked and worried me the most though. A haunting distance mixed with sadness that I so wanted to break but was afraid to. We had gotten dressed in silence, Phoenix slowly and carelessly, me stealing concerned glances at him.

It wasn't until we were walking down to my bakery, the light of the day starting to fight through the night and the clouds, that I decided to ask him. I had intertwined my fingers with his and noticed how his usually warm hand was cold and clammy, the normally tight hold slack and weak. What could he have possibly heard in the news that caused him such a reaction?

"Nix, stop for a moment." The small park we were crossing was empty. I signaled at a nearby bench and we both sat down. "What happened? What did they say on TV that upset you so much?"

Phoenix looked at me as if he was noticing me for the first time. He licked his lips and smiled—a sad smile that didn't reach his shiny eyes. "Sorry, Jo, but I think I just remembered what I was convicted for." I opened my mouth, but no words came out. "No wonder they have exacted such a severe punishment on me. I did the worst thing a guardian angel can do."

"You were a guardian angel?" Asmodeus had claimed that much, but I couldn't be sure he had been telling the truth. "What did you do?" *Oh God. Please don't tell me he killed someone.*

Phoenix lowered his eyes to our hands. "I fell in love with my charge." My stomach lurched. I had no right to be jealous—whatever happened was way before we met. "He was the artist they were talking about on TV, Anthony Mello."

Maybe I should have been surprised he'd been in love with another man, but my time with Sky had taught me that angels truly followed the philosophy of "love is love." I had asked Sky once whether there were gay angels, and he told me angels just loved purely. There was no male or female when it came to loving in the angelic world. Angel love transcended sexuality.

I gulped, trying not to reveal the nagging jealousy gnawing at my heart. "How is that a crime? Aren't angels supposed to love above all else?"

He sighed and looked up at me again. "Yes, but a guardian angel is there to make sure his charge is safe and sound. I was so distracted by our love affair that I failed to notice he was extremely depressed. Jo, I failed to prevent him from committing suicide. I lost my charge."

Earlier when we were still in bed, I hadn't been paying attention to the news. Being beside Phoenix, especially when our bare skin was touching, was extremely distracting, and I was incapable of focusing on anything else other than him and how he made my heart flutter and my skin tingle. Could he be right? Had he been punished for sleeping at work, so to speak?

I made a move for his hand. He was cold, as if all his blood had stopped running through his body. "No, it was not your fault." It seemed as if angels were not so different from humans in certain things. Suicide was hard on anyone connected to the victim—parents, siblings, spouses, friends all felt guilty for something that was out of their control. "Nix, you couldn't have known. That's the thing about suicide; you never know when someone gets that close to the edge."

"I was his guardian angel, Jo, tasked with keeping him safe until his time was up." Tears danced in his eyes, the corner of his lips drooping with each word. "He was what the angels call an 'at risk' human. That's why I was there, to make sure he didn't meet with an untimely death. And what did I do instead? I had been so blinded by my own happiness that I didn't see him slipping closer and closer to the abyss. I deserved all the pain Asmodeus inflicted on me. Every bit of it."

I pulled him in for a hug. "Nix, no. You are wrong." What could

I say to change his mind? "You made a mistake, that's all. You have a kind heart with no darkness in it whatsoever. I'm so glad you're in my life. I love you, and you make me happy every day by just being you. You certainly don't deserve the pain that evil creature exacted on you, or to be doomed for eternity."

Phoenix's head was nestled in the crook of my neck. I felt rather than heard him say, "Thank you for saying that, Jo. Thank you for loving me. I will carry the memory of you in my heart to hold me for the rest of my penance."

Cradling the back of his head with my hand, I brushed my lips against his temple. "Don't talk as if we'll never see each other again," I said, shaking and choking on my words and unshed tears. "I won't go down without a fight. I'll find a way." What way, I had no idea. "What will they do when Gabriel comes to get you?"

He seemed to have found some strength, because he lifted his head and gazed into my eyes, keeping his focused and steady. "Nothing really. I will be assigned to another master and continue to pluck souls."

An idea was percolating in my brain. "Is there such a thing as a court of appeals in heaven?" I asked, biting the inside of my face. He looked at me, eyebrows arching in question. "Can an angel or someone make an appeal to the court of the Cherubim? For another trial? If there were enough new witnesses or evidence to warrant a second look at your case?"

"I don't know. You'd have to ask Gabriel." He straightened his back. "Why? What are you thinking?"

A smile crept to my lips at the same time a shiver ran through me. I was about to ask to stand as a witness in angelic court. I wondered if this had ever happened. A human stepping in to defend an angel? I didn't care. I could be loud and annoying enough to wear down even a seraphic creature with powers I could only imagine. The long years of badgering my brother to get what I wanted would come in handy now.

# NIX

"But why, Gabriel? Why?"

I could hear Joan's voice coming through the door of my room, where I hid to give them some privacy. I had no idea what she was trying, but the discussion had been pretty heated for the past half hour or so. At first, I could barely hear Gabriel as he used his peaceful voice, the one he reserved for those he thought were being unreasonable and whose intellect and wisdom paled in comparison with his. At least, that was what Sky told me as we sat on the edge of my bed, patiently waiting for whatever came out of that conversation.

"You are being a stubborn mule, and you know it." Joan's voice reached me loud and clear. Definitely loud. My girlfriend was losing her patience. "Give me one good reason why I can't stand witness to his character and behavior. One. Good. Reason."

"The court doesn't deal with mortals." Gabriel's words were

punctuated with irritation and a lot more audible than a few minutes ago. "We cannot break with tradition—"

"Fuck the court." Uh-oh. Joan had reached the cursing stage, a sure indication she was about to lose her cookies. "You tell those motherf—"

"Sis! Watch your mouth." It was Caleb, once again coming to the rescue of those who were the target of his sister's wrath. "Be respectful. A filthy mouth never took anyone anywhere worth going."

"Oh shut up, Caleb. I am a grown woman and I can cuss to my heart's delight." Despite the situation, Sky chuckled under his breath and then threw me an apologetic glance. "The truth, Gabriel, is that you don't want to bother. The least you could do is talk to them, try to get them to see my way. Nix has atoned for his trespass over and over again. Not only was he tortured daily for twenty-five years, but he has risked his life to protect me. Don't you think that deserves some kind of reward?"

"He did that because he fell in love with you." Gabriel didn't sound so sure of himself anymore. My mouth was gritty and dry. I swallowed whatever thread of moisture still lingered on my tongue.

"Does it matter? The important thing is that he did it without anyone making him or even asking him," Joan said, her voice a bit shrill. "He knew that Asmodeus would make him pay dearly for protecting me, and yet he did it anyway. He acted as the angel of light he is, not this dark creature you are making him to be."

There was silence and I glanced at Sky, who shrugged. "Give it a moment. Joan can be very persuasive when she sets her mind to it.

And she is extremely motivated right now." I turned my eyes back to the door, wishing angels had X-ray vision.

"I can't promise you anything, but I will talk to the court." My mouth dropped open. Gabriel had actually agreed with Joan? Maybe Asmodeus was not wrong after all; maybe Joan was indeed gifted with some special talent to manipulate angelic creatures. "In the meantime, I have to take him with me. I promise I will hold him in Arcadia until a decision is made instead of taking him back to the Fortress."

Arcadia was the city of the angels of light. Now that my memory had cleared, I remembered my home there. Even though we were both Third Sphere angels, as a guardian angel, I was in a class above Sky's. I lived in Cloud Nine, an enviable celestial neighborhood among all angels. I remembered my place as a bright small space with white feathery furnishings enveloped in soothing music that always lulled me into a semi-slumber after a long day at work.

"One more day," Joan pleaded. "My bakery opened today, and we haven't had time to properly celebrate. I want to take him out one last time with Sky and Caleb. What's one more day?"

"Sorry, Joan. I already stretched it to the max," Gabriel said. "He has to come with me today. I'll give you another hour or so to say your goodbyes, but nothing more."

The word goodbye hit me with the force of a well-thrown punch. I gasped for air but made myself whisper a thank-you for the little time we still had left. Sky placed a hand on my shoulder and gave it a gentle squeeze. I looked at him and attempted a smile but failed miserably.

"I know Joan," he said, his hand still grasping my shoulder. "She won't give up on you. You couldn't have a better champion."

The door opened and Gabriel came through, a bright white halo around him. "I'll be back in a while to get you. Be ready."

He turned around and my view was replaced by the one face I loved more than anything in the world. I immediately forgot about everything else and pounced to my feet, already running to her.

"I will fight for you to the end," she said, her voice muffled by my shirt. "I love you, Nix."

I had no doubt she would, but my faith in her didn't extend to faith in the Cherubim, not well known for their empathy or mercy toward other creatures, including other angels. This could well be the last hour I had with my human, and I didn't want to waste it talking about my situation. I wanted to wrap myself around her lovely body, inhale her, and keep her in my heart forever. Whatever tomorrow brought, no one could take these memories from me.

# CHAPTER 12
## THE COUNCIL

## JOAN

The black and white stripes of the canopy over my storefront didn't improve when I squinted, but I liked the way the darker colors merged with the lighter in a blurry but pretty watercolor. It reminded me of Phoenix, my angel who was both dark and light. Not for the first time that day, I wondered how he was doing, alone and captive in Arcadia while the Cherubim decided his fate. Sky had told me about the detention cells where he spent some time himself and how the sensory deprivation was the worst part of it. That and the constant fear of what may happen next.

I shook my head and walked in. I hadn't heard from Gabriel in a couple weeks, and despite my state of unrest and anxiety, life went on, and I had a business to run. Shedding my coat, I hung it up on the coatrack before heading to the counter where Tess was busy rearranging the pastries and cookies in the glass display. After a long day at work, I always joined her at the bakery until it closed at six. Tess sometimes stayed and helped me with preparations for the next day, but more often than not, I enjoyed the solitude the closed store provided.

"Here's the boss," Tess exclaimed, giving me an exaggerated wave. The store was empty except for an older couple seated by the window. "How was your day at work?"

I came around to stand by her behind the counter and tied an apron around my waist. Tess had gifted me with a set of cottony black aprons printed with the name of the bakery—a name I had changed at the last minute to Dark Angel Cookies—in white.

"Long. I can't wait to be able to fully dedicate myself to the bakery." Lately, I was so distracted it was a miracle I hadn't been fired yet. "How did business go today?"

"Good, actually," Tess said, artistically staging a pile of white chocolate chip cookies on a small black stand. "We ran out of the snickerdoodles and chocolate chip. You would think there was a shortage of cookies in the world." She laughed. "There was this older guy—handsome and grumpy—that bought most of them."

That caught my attention. "Did he pay cash?" Gabriel always paid cash. Something to do with angels and their aversion to credit cards. He was the only one I knew who would be willing to shell out that kind of money for my cookies. "You didn't happen to catch his name, did you?"

"No, sorry. But he did say he would be back later to talk to you." Tess bit her lower lip. "He's not some kind of stalker, is he? Because I can kick his ass if you want." She probably could. Tess worked out every morning before coming to open the store, a strict regimen of weight lifting and kickboxing.

"He's not dangerous. Just an old friend of the family." Not that I would describe him as a friend. Maybe an ally and definitely a pain in the ass, but I really wanted to talk to him. "You can take off, Tess. I'll take it from here."

"I have a date with Ally. I'm not sure she's the one, but I'm having fun with her." Tess washed her hands, hung her apron on the hook on the wall, gave me a hug, and left.

The two customers left, and the store was empty of life beside me. I wiped the tables, refilled the sugar caddies, checked the supplies, and washed the espresso machine, which this late in the day was rarely required. I opened the stepladder and climbed until I could reach the large black chalkboard behind the counter. With a wet rag, I wiped the specials menu and waited for it to dry so I could write the one for the next day. I always took great pains to do it in cute, artsy handwriting with my old-fashioned white chalk.

"I love what you've done to the place."

I almost fell off the ladder. I braced myself on the wall before turning my head in the direction of the voice. "Could you possibly be any creepier?" I gingerly climbed down the two steps and popped the chalk inside my pocket. "I could have killed myself."

Gabriel was standing by the counter, tall, blond, and handsome despite the permanent grumpiness etched in his expression. He raised one single eyebrow—how did he do that?—and cleared his throat. "It's not my fault you had your head in the clouds." He gave me a self-satisfied smile.

Even though I was annoyed, I was more interested in finding out what was going on with my angel. "How's Phoenix? Any news?"

"He's fine." His eyes roamed over the cookies in the display shelf and his tongue flickered over his lips. "No more of the chocolate chip?"

I shook my head. "No. Can we go back to talking about Nix? What's going on?" Why couldn't the damn archangel forget about his gluttony for a second?

"The court has agreed to listen to your testimony." My knees shook and the room swayed. "This is unheard of, Joan. No human has ever been allowed to speak for an angel. I hope you realize what a privilege you are being offered by the Cherubim."

Privilege, my ass. But I didn't want to jeopardize my chances, so I would play nice. "I will never be able to thank you enough, Gabriel," I said. "I will pledge a lifetime supply of chocolate chip cookies to you as a thank-you."

Gabriel's chest plumped up like that of a rooster. "This is no promise of anything beyond the hearing, you understand."

"I know, but I'm still thankful for the opportunity." I was being sincere now. Gabriel had kept his promise and taken the matter to the high order of the Cherubim, a group of angels that, according to Sky, was not the nicest or most sympathetic. God only knew what strings he had to pull to accomplish that. "When is the hearing?"

"Soon. I will have a team of angel techs come to install the necessary connections for the hearing."

I blinked. "Connections? What are you talking about? Aren't you going to take me to Arcadia?"

A burst of laughter made me flinch. "You can't go to Arcadia," Gabriel said in between chuckles. "It will be a virtual testimony."

"Will I see Phoenix?" I missed him so bad it hurt. "I want to see him and make sure he's being treated fairly."

Gabriel frowned, taking a hand to his chest. "Of course he's being treated fairly," he said, a note of outrage in his voice. "We're angels, not demons."

I twisted my lips to one side, my eyebrows knitted tightly between my eyes. "Right, as if that has ever stopped a few of you from being cruel."

Even though his wings were retracted, I could almost see his feathers quivering in indignation. "There are a few of us that go rogue, but those are the exceptions to the rule. Angels strive at doing what's right and with love behind every action."

I nodded, not wanting to enrage him any further. He was Phoenix's only ally in Arcadia, after all. "Sorry, Gabriel. I'm mad that Nix is in jail when he did nothing but what was right while Asmodeus is probably still having fun torturing souls."

Gabriel flinched at my words, and a wicked part of me smiled in satisfaction. It couldn't be easy to admit to himself that angels were not perfect.

"Anyway, will I see him?"

"Not sure," he admitted with a shake of his head. "The

Cherubim are not very forthcoming with information, you know." No, of course I didn't know. Yes, I had an angel for a soon-to-be brother-in-law, but I doubted that he knew much about the higher echelon of the angelic world. "We'll have to wait and find out when the day comes."

Panic rose in my chest. Angels didn't have a clear understanding of time, not being mortal and all that. What they thought of as soon could be years off. "This is going to be in the next week or so, right?"

"In three days," Gabriel said. "My team should arrive at your house within a day or so." He seemed as if he was ready to go when he turned to me again and added, "Please don't feed my angels. I don't want them distracted by your cookies."

It wasn't until I watched him disappear without as much as a poof that I noticed he had taken a whole plate full of cookies I had placed on the table closest to him. Jerk!

## NIX

The thumping of my own heart echoed in my ears and seemed to bounce off the walls, ricocheting over my head, my clipped wings, and the empty white space around me. I hadn't heard a sound or seen another soul in days. It was hard to tell how much time had passed in that room, a white, padded cube with no visual references of any kind. In many ways this was similar to Asmodeus's chamber of horrors, except here I knew I wouldn't be tortured or played with.

I figured that was a major improvement, though isolation was not much better. It didn't mess with me physically, but it sure was doing a number with my head.

"I didn't know, Anthony I really missed it."

Anthony had been visiting me for the past few days. I knew it was a hallucination or something along those lines. Despite popular belief, angels could not see dead people. Once the souls were free from their bodies, they were carried to Arcadia's repository by the angels of death and never seen again by any of us lowly angels. Anthony was something else, probably a product of my guilty conscience now that I remembered what had happened.

"I'm so sorry, Anthony. I should have seen it." Anthony sat across the room, his back against the wall, wearing the same clothes he had been wearing the last time I'd seen him that fateful day. "When you left the studio, I was so full of happiness, I forgot what my job was. I forgot I was to shadow you every minute of the day and make sure you were safe." I swallowed. My mouth was desert arid. "I was so sure you were as happy as I was that I missed the clues. And there were many, so many…."

The vision of my former lover smiled at me as he brushed his fingers through his blond hair. "I was happy, my angel, just not enough to stick around. I was ready to let go of this world." His eyes were as blue as I remembered, the color of the azure pigment he used in so many of his paintings. "I'm happy now, sweet angel. So happy."

It was a figment of my imagination, I knew, but it was still soothing to hear him say those words. Ever since my memories returned, guilt had suffocated me, a poisonous snake coiling itself around my heart and soul.

"I loved you," I heard myself say. I had loved him with all the power of my angelic body and soul and had fooled myself into believing I could have him for eternity. "It hurts to think my love was not enough to hold you to life, but it hurts me even more that I failed in my mission as a guardian angel. I'm sorry."

"You're sorry for what, angel?" I was so focused on Anthony that I hadn't seen Gabriel walk in, his white wings blending seamlessly with the walls and floor.

I jumped to my feet, cringing as the wing clips pinched tighter behind my back. I wasn't going to let him see me sweat. Since Anthony's suicide, I had lived my life as a lower-than-dirt creature, spineless and scared of its own shadow. No matter what happened, from now on I would stand tall and accept the consequences of my actions as the being of love I was.

"I have news for you—em, Phoenix." Gabriel was still having trouble using my chosen name. I wondered if he knew my real one. That was one memory I had not recovered and was not sorry I hadn't; Phoenix was the name Joan knew me by and therefore the one I would always answer to.

I took a few hesitant steps toward him, the nipping of my wings stunting my every move. "Good or bad?" My attempt at levity didn't quite work, and my voice caught in my throat.

"The Cherubim have agreed to a retrial," Gabriel said, much to my surprise. "They will listen to Joan's testimony and take it under advisement when deciding what to do with you."

Being talked about as a pawn on a chess board rubbed me the wrong way, and I had to bite my tongue to avoid saying something I would certainly regret later. Gabriel was a pompous ass, but he was doing what he could to help me and Joan. Maybe underneath all those peacock feathers there was a sympathetic warm heart after all.

"They are allowing her in Arcadia?" That would be unheard of. In fact, I was not even sure it was possible.

"No, no, that can't be." Gabriel scoffed, shaking his head like a mating flamingo. "It will all happen virtually. My team is on Earth as we speak, setting everything up. The trial is scheduled for tomorrow."

I tried to swallow, but the knot in my throat wouldn't let me. "What can I expect?"

Gabriel waved his hand and a couple soft chairs appeared out of nowhere. He invited me to sit before sitting himself. "You will be allowed to watch the whole thing but not allowed to speak," the archangel explained. "Joan will be asked to address the court and say whatever she wants to say on your behalf, after which the Cherubim will adjourn for a while to discuss it. They may ask her some questions." He looked up at me, his light blue eyes revealing an intelligence that belied his usual crankiness and vanity. "It's rare, but they may also ask you some questions."

"What kind of questions?" The urge to reach behind my back to remove the restraints that dug into me every time I moved was strong, but I knew it wouldn't do any good. Those things didn't come out that easily.

"I would stick to your relationship with Joan and not mention Anthony," he said, getting up and walking behind me to check my wings. "Does it hurt?" I nodded. "I will loosen it up a bit." I didn't feel his hands, but the relief was immediate. I was still bound, but I could now move without feeling the bite of the clips. "With Anthony you messed up big-time. With Joan you had no idea of your past trespasses and risked your own skin to protect her. That may count for something."

The uncertainty of his words was not comforting or promising, but having a chance, however minimal, was worth more than I could express. "Thank you, Gabriel." He nodded and stood up to go. "How's Jo?"

He turned his head back to me. "She's fine. The business is thriving, and she has a loving brother and good friends to keep her afloat." I sighed in relief. "But she misses you, Phoenix. She's willing to do whatever it takes to protect you the way you protected her. She's a keeper." Then he was gone along with his chair.

The flames of yearning flared in my chest and gut—yearning for Joan's love, the life together we could never have, my best and only friend. I dropped to my knees and vaguely acknowledged the vanishing chair as I released the tears I had been holding in.

# CHAPTER 13
## THE TRIAL

## JOAN

The level of technical complexity of whatever system the angels had installed in my house was astounding, more so because these were divine beings who I'd expected not to need any of these more mundane tools. That said, the fact that I would be connecting to celestial beings who lived in a totally different dimension had to require some mumbo jumbo.

I watched as the last of the techy angels unfurled her wings and vanished, leaving me finally alone. There were no wires connecting any of the deceitfully simple items that had been installed in my living room, but the focus was on this ethereal veil-like screen stretched over my main wall. I had sneaked a feel earlier and was amazed by it—soft and yet firm, solid but not. What was that stuff made of?

I had taken the day off from my day job and also from the bakery. Tess had offered to hold the fort and promised to drop some chicken soup after closing while I recovered from a fictitious cold. I didn't say no since I expected to be done with the trial procedures by then. Gabriel had told me angelic trials didn't last long. I sat on the couch and stared at the screen, not sure what to expect. Would it crackle like an old radio to let me know the connection was established, or would it suddenly light up with images of these Cherubim creatures? I wondered what they would look like. The only Cherubim I knew were the silly depictions in art of those chubby naked babies hovering over humans. Would they be naked? God, I hoped not. It wouldn't bode well for my case if I couldn't keep a straight face during the testimony.

"Are you ready, Joan?" Gabriel sneaked up on me as usual. "The trial is about to start."

I gulped and licked my lips, certain that no matter how long I had, I would never be truly prepared to testify in a celestial court. "As ready as I will ever be. Let's get this show on the road."

Gabriel threw me a quizzical look and sat beside me. "I was told to stick by you during the trial and make sure nothing goes awry on this side of things." Great, an angelic chaperone. My brother would approve of it.

Sky had tried to get permission to stand by me, but Gabriel dug in his heels and refused to let him, so he was at home with Caleb, anxiously waiting to hear from me. Their wedding was just around the corner, and I felt guilty that I wasn't there for them much lately.

The screen briefly shimmered and the figures of three angels appeared. They were not what I expected at all. These angels were as tall as all the others I had ever seen, but it was impossible to guess their gender. They wore robes of light, a soft glow that enveloped their bodies, obscuring any gender identifiers, and their wings seemed to be covered in mother-of-pearl that caught every ray of light and reflected it in every direction. Their hair, if they had any, was indiscernible from behind the curtain of light the Cherubim emitted. They all sat on a dais, which appeared to consist only of clouds, in throne chairs with their hands resting on their thighs, waiting.

"Are you the one named Joan?" The voice, genderless and imposing, exploded in my ears. I flinched and stared at the screen, trying to figure out which of them was talking. "Speak up, child."

The tone left no margin for resistance. "Yes, your—" What should I call them? Your Cherubimness? Your Honor didn't seem right.

"We understand you want to give testimony in favor of the former guardian angel you know as Phoenix. Is that correct?"

Try as I might, I couldn't see their lips moving. Hell, I couldn't see any lips. "Yes, that's correct."

"You have the floor to make your case," the cherub said.

I looked at the screen, frantically searching for Phoenix, but I couldn't see him anywhere. I wondered whether he was watching. I swallowed the bile that had risen to my mouth and tried to appear calm and collected as I looked straight at the Cherubim.

"I know that Phoenix was charged and convicted for a serious transgression as a guardian angel." I had been practicing the speech since Gabriel told me I would be giving testimony. "He was blinded by love and lowered his guard just long enough to lose his charge. I know it has been at least twenty-five years since this happened, years of great pain and torment for Phoenix at the hands of Asmodeus."

As far as I could tell, there was no reaction from any of the Cherubim, who listened without interrupting or moving. Gabriel shifted beside me and briefly touched my shoulder as if to encourage me. How unlike him.

"For twenty-five years Phoenix was beaten, raped, and tortured in every possible way by his cruel master, all the while not having a clue as to what he was being punished for," I continued, anger growing in my chest as I recalled all that had happened to my angel. "This, I believe, is against all seraphic laws, and yet it was allowed to continue for years. Phoenix was robbed of his own memories and condemned to unimaginable pain. However, he was willing to risk his own well-being to save me, to protect me from his master. Phoenix knew he would be severely punished, but he still did it."

I stole a glance at Gabriel, who smiled and nodded. "He didn't do it because he thought it would be a way of convincing the upper echelon to forgive him; he had no memory of what had happened to him. He did it because he loved me more than he loved himself. He did it because deep inside, he is still the selfless guardian angel he was before. Phoenix did this because he's a creature made of love."

A quiet rumbling of what I thought were voices vibrated in my ears. "I beg you to forgive him. He has more than atoned for his crime. Don't punish him for doing what angels were created to do—

love unconditionally." I stopped for effect and to gather courage to say what I was about to say, words that stirred the jealousy monster inside of me, but it had to be said. "Anthony Mello chose to quit living on his own, but Phoenix made his last days on Earth the happiest he probably ever had. Isn't that worth something?"

The rumbling grew, and Gabriel squeezed my hand over the seat as if to signal me to wrap it up. "And he made my life so much richer and exciting and worth living because of his love." I lowered my eyes, tears burning behind my lashes. "This is my testimony, my request for mercy. I thank you for the opportunity and for the honor."

The screen wavered a bit. "Thank you for your testimony, child. We will consider all you said and make a decision."

Without any more words, the screen went blank and all angelic technology fizzled out and died. I released a long exhale of air that had been burning my insides.

"You did well, Joan," Gabriel said, uncharacteristically sympathetic. "They will decide quickly, within the day." He stood up. "I will send a couple angels to clean this up, and as soon as I know anything, I will send word."

As usual I didn't have time to thank him before he vanished, a little residual light lingering behind where he had stood.

How could I be so tired from simply talking? I felt as if I had run a marathon, and even though I should've been calling Caleb and Sky, I curled up on the couch, pulled a throw over myself, and closed my eyes. I didn't want to wake up until Phoenix was free, so I let exhaustion take me under the blissful peace of slumber.

# NIX

Anthony came to visit one more time. To say goodbye, or so I thought. He smiled at me, tapped that silly white hat he always wore, and threw me a kiss before walking away and disappearing into the white walls of my cell. Guilt would never leave me, but I'd had some closure in that small room, deprived of sensory stimulation of any kind other than my own thoughts and my imagination. I waved at the emptiness he had left behind and then dropped my hand on my lap. The Cherubim had not announced their decision yet, but I wasn't too hopeful. I had resigned myself to a life as a dark angel, doing the menial job of plucking souls. And never seeing Joan again.

I hung my head and willed myself to sleep. As an angel, I didn't need much sleep, but I had quickly found that I could use it to ward against the solitude of the holding cell. In my dreams I could talk to Joan, touch and love her the way I couldn't in reality.

"They have made a decision, Phoenix." Gabriel snapped me out of my half-sleep. He stood by the door, his mighty wings unfurled and spread to their full width. A formidable sight. "Follow me."

Afraid of what the answer might be, I didn't ask the question burning on my lips: What had they decided? I stood up and did what he told me. The light outside blinded me for a moment. The warmth of the sun caressed my bare arms and I took a deep breath, enjoying the fresh and flower-scented air of Arcadia. I remembered it well.

Gabriel led me across the market square toward a large building that I recognized as the headquarters of the Death Squad. Sky had once worked there, I knew. The big transparent front door opened as we approached, and the archangel took me up the wide spiral stairs into an office I didn't recognize but guessed was his. Eyes followed us all the way up, their scrutiny and curiosity burning a hole in my back. "There goes the guardian angel who let his charge kill himself," they seemed to say. "What a stupid, unworthy angel."

He closed what stood for a door but was nothing more than a translucent curtain and came around behind me. I was sure the others could see us through the nonexistent walls, but it was still a relief.

"I'm unclipping your wings, Phoenix," he announced unnecessarily as a snap preceded an amazing sense of freedom; my wings were free again. I wanted to unfurl and stretch them to get rid of the cramping and kinks the clips left behind, but I wasn't sure I should. Gabriel faced me again and waved a hand. "Go on, unfurl them."

It was hard to explain what I felt as I stretched my black wings, one feather at a time. Joan always sighed in delight when she got home and took off her shoes. "It's torture having to keep my toes inside these dressy shoes," she'd say. "My toesies need freedom." Then she would open and fan her toes with moans and squeaks of delight. I imagined it was the same kind of feeling I had when I finally opened my wings to their full span.

"Sit down." Gabriel pointed at the chair in front of his desk, a clean and organized surface of some crystal-like material that allowed light through. I did as he said, adjusting my wings around the back of the chair so I didn't have to retract them again. It felt too good to have them open. "As you probably guessed, there will be some changes to your status."

My heart shrank. This was the part I had been fearing the most. What would they do to me? I knew it couldn't be any worse than serving under Asmodeus. But being a dark angel, especially now that I had regained my memory of better days, was still a cruel sentence. Not being able to be with Joan only added more pain to the whole thing. I was made to save souls, not take them to eternal agony.

"You will be reassigned as of right now," Gabriel said in a matter-of-fact tone, as if my fate was purely a routine event. "You will be given a night to recover, and then you'll be sent to your new assignment."

I couldn't bring myself to ask where this new assignment was. I glanced around me as if some magical door would suddenly open for me to escape whatever was waiting for me. I twisted my hands on my lap until my knuckles were sore and my breath came out ragged.

"Well, that's all for now, angel," Gabriel said, standing up. "One of my aides will take you to your quarters for the night."

I stood up as he headed to the door. Wasn't he going to tell me where I was going? "With all respect, Gabriel," I said, swallowing my fear, "you haven't told me where I'm being assigned to."

Gabriel opened his eyes wide. "I haven't?" He scratched his head. "I apologize. It's been a crazy few days. I thought I already told you."

Shaking my head wildly, I waited anxiously for his answer. "No, you didn't say anything."

To my great surprise, the archangel took a step toward me and laid a hand on my shoulder. He was about the same height as me, and his blue eyes locked on mine. "Phoenix, you are being assigned to an earthbound position." What did that mean? I had never heard of it. Confusion must have been obvious in my eyes, because he explained, "You will be our eyes and ears on Earth for some years. You're to follow the angelic code of conduct at all times and report to us anytime you're asked to."

Still confused, I licked my lips blinking rapidly. "I don't understand."

He lowered his voice and bent down slightly so his face was closer to mine. "You will be on Earth, free to be with Joan if you choose to do so." I went weak in the knees and he had to steady me. "The court decided that you had indeed not only atoned for your crime but went far beyond what you were expected to do. You will be reinstated as an angel of light and work on Earth as a social worker specially assigned for at-risk teens."

I couldn't believe my ears. I was going to be allowed to stay with Joan and be an angel of light again? "Is this true, Gabriel? Are you teasing me?"

"No teasing, I promise." Gabriel smiled, a rather rare occurrence. "You will be able to stay with Joan for as long as you want as an earthbound angel of light."

"Like Sky." I knew his story—every angel in Arcadia and the Fortress knew his story—but I never thought to ask how come he had been allowed to stay with Caleb. I assumed it was due to his disability, his missing wings, but now I was beginning to question that.

"Yes, like Sky." Gabriel squeezed my shoulder, an oddly friendly gesture coming from someone who was not generally viewed as such. "There are others. Some come back once their human mates pass; others choose to remain earthbound."

Could it be? Was I still inside the white cell, hallucinating or dreaming? "Does Joan know?" It was a squeak rather than a question.

Gabriel dropped his hand. "No, I thought you'd like to do that yourself." An angel appeared at the door to lead me to my quarters. Gabriel nodded toward him. "Ariel will take you to your room. I strongly suggest you rest before you fly to Earth, but you're free to go whenever you're ready."

I stuttered a string of thank-yous and followed the angel Ariel in stunned silence.

I was going home.

# CHAPTER 14
## THE WEDDING

## JOAN

"Those wings look weird there," Sky said, a hand cupping his chin. "Maybe over the pergola."

He may have been an angel, but Sky was also the fussiest decorator in the world. We'd been trying to set up their wedding venue for hours, and it seemed as if all we were doing was shuffling objects around.

"You better be sure this time," I warned him, a murderous tinge in my voice. "I'm not moving these fucking wings one more time."

"Watch your mouth, sis." The usual and expected comment from my brother made me smile. I was so happy for him, even though he could be such a shithead sometimes. "You're in the presence of a divine being."

I snorted. "Divine, my ass. I love you, Sky, but divine is going a bit too far."

Sky laughed and pulled Caleb closer to him. "But I love that Caleb thinks I am."

Who could argue with that? I wished I had my own angel right then with me, divine or not. I shook my head, refusing to let sadness intrude on the joy of the occasion. My one and only brother was tying the knot with an angel from heaven. Literally. I couldn't be happier to welcome Sky into our tiny family. He had become a brother to me since he knocked at our door that evening a few years ago in search of the mortal he had saved and fallen in love with a few days earlier. That day will go down in history as a pivotal point in our lives. That was the day my brother quit being an old man in the body of a twentysomething and began living again.

I balanced myself on top of the ladder and stretched over the arched white pergola that was serving as a wedding altar of sorts to position the beautiful fake angel wings Gabriel had generously offered as a wedding gift. Either there was more to the archangel than he let on, or he was still feeling guilty for having accused Sky of a crime he hadn't committed.

Caleb and Sky kept chattering behind me, giggling like elementary school girls and gifting each other with kisses. They were such dorks. But cute though. It was the sudden silence that alerted me. I braced myself on the top of the ladder, turned slightly to see what was happening, and then almost fell. Standing next to my brother and his fiancé was the one creature I loved the most in this world.

"Nix!" Was it really him, or was I having some kind of hallucination brought on by my extreme yearning and sadness? He smiled sheepishly and didn't move. "Is it really you? Caleb, are you seeing the same thing I'm seeing?"

Caleb chuckled. "Yes, fool. Phoenix is here. Will you climb off that ladder and come welcome him?"

I dropped the wings and they fell on a couple of storage boxes with a loud thump that didn't bode well for their contents. Leaping off the steps, I flew into Phoenix's arms and buried my face in the crook of his neck. With a laugh, Phoenix spun me around, my feet flying off the floor as if I weighed nothing.

When we finally stopped, I was still hanging from his neck, unwilling to let go of him. "Tell me you're here to stay, Nix," I whispered against his skin, my lips delighting in his warmth. "I don't think I can stand seeing you leave again."

He kissed the side of my head. "I'm here to stay, Jo. Not going anywhere any time soon."

I lifted my head and sought his lips with the greed of the starved. The world dissipated around us, and for a moment we were the center of the universe. "I love you so much, Nix."

"I love you too," he whispered over my lips.

"I hate to interrupt this lovefest, but we have a wedding to plan and a room to decorate." Caleb's crooked smile made me laugh. He stepped closer to us and stretched his hand out to Phoenix. "Welcome back, man. We're very happy to have you back."

"And now we have a couple of extra hands to help us out with this wedding," Sky added, his face so serious I couldn't help it; I burst out laughing. "What? It's true, right?"

"We probably should give them a minute alone." Caleb risked a sideways glance at his angelic fiancé, who had turned into a slave master these past few days.

As much as I wanted to get out of there and sequester myself in my room with Phoenix for a lovemaking marathon, this was also my brother's moment, and I didn't want to spoil it. The wedding was set for this weekend, a mere four days away, and there was still a lot to be done.

I looked up at Phoenix's gorgeous face and smiled. "Give us half an hour to talk over coffee, and we'll be all yours, right, Nix?"

Phoenix's serious face opened into the sunniest smile ever. "I'd love to help," he said. "There's no hurry. We have a lifetime ahead of us."

Those few words made me irrationally happy. Did that mean he could stay with me? I licked my lips and stared at him, waiting for a confirmation to my unspoken question. He nodded and I couldn't hold it any longer; I yelped and kissed him again, long and hard.

We talked over coffee at a coffeeshop down the street from the wedding site. He told me everything that had happened, and I expressed how frustrated I'd been with the silence from Gabriel and his higher-ups. "But I forgive them all, now that you're here," I declared magnanimously.

By the time we went back to join my brother, we had surely broken the record for the most kisses and hugs in less than an hour. I couldn't keep my hands off him, afraid he would vanish again, so we held hands even when we resumed decorating for my brother's wedding day. Try as I might, I couldn't focus on the task at hand; my thoughts were fully occupied by what Phoenix and I would be doing that night. Together forever at last.

## NIX

"We're going home." Joan's emphatic statement made Caleb smile. "You're on your own for the rest of the night. You can go home and have wild monkey sex for all I care. I'm taking Nix home."

Caleb leaned over and whispered in my ear. "Do you have condoms?" Oddly enough, I cringed.

Recovering quickly, I told him, "No need, Caleb. Angels don't carry disease and can't procreate with humans." He blanched a bit, though I was not sure if out of shock or surprise. "You, better than anyone, should know that."

Caleb turned to Sky and exclaimed, "If angels don't carry disease why have we used condoms all this time?"

Sky looked baffled. "Is that what they are for?" he asked. Joan snickered under her breath. "I thought that was some kind of human ritual, so I went along with it."

Joan's brother slapped his forehead, and Joan burst out laughing. "Heaven help us. You have to love these two," she said, wiping a tear from the corner of her eye. Caleb was still glaring at Sky, who looked as confused as I was about the levity of the condom issue.

Taking advantage of the momentary distraction, Joan held my hand as she pulled me toward the door and we made our escape. The sun had long descended into its resting place, and the moon shone gloriously in a cloudless sky. The star-studded black velvet of the sky seemed to mimic the way I felt—soft, yielding, and shining. I walked on the hard sidewalks as if I were walking on a cloud; for a moment, I thought I may have been floating, but my feet were solidly on the ground. Happiness seemed to give me a pair of extra wings.

Joan stopped every so often and pulled me to her for a kiss. My legs had turned soft and malleable as other areas of my body had turned rock hard. I quickened my step, wanting to get to our place sooner. Our place. There was a poetic tone to those words so I repeated them to Joan. "Can't wait to get to our place."

She squeezed my hand in hers. "I love the sound of that—our place, our home," she said in a singsong voice. "Let's run. I'm in urgent need of some angelic TLC."

I had no idea what that was, but it sounded like something I could get into. I scooped her into my arms, unfurled my wings, and took flight.

"Are you crazy? People will see you." Joan held on to me and stared down at the earth we were leaving behind as I flew both of us to our nest.

"No they won't," I said. "We're under a charm. No one can see us right now."

Her eyes glowed with a glint of mischief. "So if we wanted to get naked and make love right here, we could and no one would see us?"

I laughed and flew a little higher, the cold air caressing each feather of my wings. "Theoretically, yes, but I don't think I could without dropping you. There are limits to what I can do, you know."

Joan slid a hand over my cheek in a caress that made me shiver in anticipation and yearning. "But you can do that thing that no one can...." She lingered on the last word before kissing my chin. "Can't wait for you to show me again." Tarnation, if I got any harder, I would explode in flight.

When we finally alit by her house, I retracted my wings and broke the charm. Passersby would not give us a second look—just two lovers walking hand in hand. The house was dark except for the soft glow of the whimsical night-lights Joan had placed around the house. One in particular caught my eye; it was in the shape of a pair of dark wings in flight and emitted a flickering red light that resembled flames.

Joan caught my eye. "I found it in a store by the harbor a few days ago," she explained, leaning in and propping her arms up on my shoulders, her head barely reaching even on her tiptoes. "It's a phoenix being reborn from the ashes. Like you." Her last words were uttered in a whisper that brought tears to my eyes.

I turned and pulled her against my chest, where my heart was so full, I could hardly breathe. "You know that's not my real name, right?" I whispered, my lips grazing the top of her head. "I couldn't remember it, so I made one up on the spot."

"Something inside you knew that name would fit you to a tee," she said, her face scrunched against my thumping heart. "That is your name, Nix, one hundred percent yours."

Even though my memory was fully recovered, I couldn't recall my name. Gabriel knew it and had asked me if I wanted to know it. I didn't. Phoenix was my name when I found Joan and redemption. I would stand by it and leave my former self in the past.

"I thought I'd lost you." Joan's soft voice melted my heart further. The tears that had been stinging my eyes rolled down my cheeks. I thought I'd lost her too, and the memory still burned my very soul. I held her tighter. "I love you so much, Nix."

She turned her face to me, her eyes shiny with tears too. I covered her lips with mine and indulged in a long kiss. Her hands slipped under my T-shirt and began exploring my back, her fingers tracing the ridges of my muscles, the same spots that had endured the cruelty of my master. There were no scars since angels regenerated quickly, at least not any she could see or feel. The scars were there nevertheless, never to be forgotten, but the touch of my Earth angel healed them one inch at a time every time she touched me. Whoever said mortals had no magic were fools.

I tugged at the edges of her shirt and tore it off her, pulling it over her head with an urgency that surprised me. Quickly, I removed mine, groaning at the distance it carved between us. Joan glued herself to me again, the warmth of her bare skin against mine soothing and slowing me down as I skimmed her neck with my lips, from her earlobe to her shoulder and then back again. Her whimpers only added fuel to my growing desire.

We stumbled our way to the bedroom, shedding clothing

items along the way, and by the time we fell onto the bed, not a thing separated our bodies. I latched my lips around her breast, groaning in wonder at how amazing she felt and tasted. Joan arched her upper body toward my mouth, muttering words I understood without hearing them clearly.

In a surprise move, Joan flipped me under her, and I chuckled. "You're pretty strong for such a wisp of a girl," I said, flattening my hands on her smooth back.

The crooked smile on her lips made me tremble in anticipation as she began rocking and rolling on top of me, momentarily pausing to lower herself on my arousal. She pressed herself downward and I buried myself deeper inside her, gasping and shivering in delight. We danced and came together, breaths and heartbeats entwined into one.

As we both lay blissfully exhausted, Joan collapsed over me, and it finally sank in—I was on Earth beside my love to stay.

⸸

JOAN

"Hands off! Bad, bad angel," I exclaimed, slapping Gabriel's hand off the platter of cookies I placed on the table. This archangel had a serious addiction to sugar. "That's for the reception. You can have them after the wedding."

Caleb looked up and laughed. "You better listen to her, Gabriel. Not a good idea to go against her rules, trust me."

The room was ready for my brother's wedding. White festoons hung from the walls and white roses decorated the guest chairs. The centerpiece was the latticed double-wide pergola beneath which Caleb would be pledging his forever love to an angel—not that he hadn't already. It was a small wedding. We had no family, and Caleb hadn't cultivated many friendships since my parents had been killed in the accident. Surprising everyone, Gabriel was in attendance, his tall, handsome figure clad in a blindingly white tuxedo only an angel could pull off. Tess and her girlfriend, Ally, were there, fussing over the catered food and driving the couple of servers insane. Phoenix was helping Sky get ready in the dressing room while Caleb fluttered around like a mad dragonfly, his anxiety translating into random and aimless wandering.

"Will you sit down already?" I told him. He was making me nervous, and I had no reason to be. My brother looked handsome in a classy black suit over a snow-white shirt that made the sky blue tie pop out in contrast. "You guys have been living together for over four years. It's not as if he's about to pop your cherry."

Caleb cringed. "Hell, Joan. Could you be any cruder?" I laughed at his reaction. Even after a lifetime together, he still hadn't figured out that I said those things just to get a rise out of him. "Is my tie crooked?" He pulled on the knot by his neck, effectively skewing it.

"Lord, bro. Now it is crooked." I pulled his hands away from the tie and fixed it myself. I brushed his shoulders with my hands and then planted a kiss on his cheek. "You look very spiffy, Caleb. I'm so happy for you."

Without warning, he pulled me to him and hugged me. "Thanks, sis. I still find it hard to believe we both ended up in love with angels. What are the odds?"

I laughed. "Apparently pretty good in our family," I said, pushing him gently away. "Now, can you go to your dressing room and relax? The minister will be here any second, and if you're this hyper, you won't be able to spit out your vows."

A horrified expression clouded his face. "Holy shit, the vows. I forgot about it," he exclaimed, searching his pockets for the piece of paper he had been carrying around all week. "Here it is. Thank God. Do you have the rings?"

I crossed my arms, pretending to be mad. "For God's sake, will you stop worrying about every little thing?" I held both his shoulders, spun him around, and forcefully pushed him toward the dressing room. "Go practice your vows for the millionth time. I will call you when everything is ready."

The minister arrived shortly after. We had a short chat, and then I began seating those in attendance. There were a few of Caleb's coworkers and the old lady who lived down the road who'd become their frequent visitor for the last couple years.

Once they were all sitting down, I went to knock at Sky's door. "Guys, it's time."

Phoenix cracked the door open and smiled. My heart raced immediately. That smile made my insides melt on demand. He offered me his hand, and we both walked to our spot by the pergola.

In the back, Tess turned on the music and a smile stretched my lips. Caleb had chosen Breaking Benjamin's "Angels Fall" as their wedding song. On cue, both my brother and Sky appeared, walked to the center of the room, and held hands, the goofiest and happiest smiles on their faces. Standing under the pergola, they faced the minister, a tall woman wearing a long black robe and a bright, thin red scarf draped over her shoulders.

Phoenix squeezed my hand, and I blinked back the stubborn tears prickling in my eyes. I patted the pocket of my dress, making sure the rings were still there, and then sighed.

The ceremony was short but beautiful, and soon it was time for the exchange of vows. Caleb had been very secretive about his, unlike Sky, who had requested my help to write his. When Caleb finally held on to his angel's hand and began reciting what he had jealously kept a secret, I could not hold my tears any longer.

"Of all the angels in heaven, I am loved by the best, my friend and partner, my love," my brother concluded. "Sky Heavensent, will you accept me as your husband for our eternity, however long that might be?"

Sky's lips stretched even farther. "I do, Caleb, I do. With all my heart. For eternity."

I stepped forward to hand them their rings and stole a quick—and totally out of place—kiss from the two grooms. They exchanged the rings and then locked eyes. There was so much love in their gazes, I had to stop myself from clapping hysterically.

"You may kiss now."

As they locked lips, Phoenix pulled me closer to him and

whispered, "I love you too." I held on to his arm as if afraid he may run away. "Don't be alarmed," he added. "Sky and I prepared a little surprise; only you and your brother will see."

I didn't have time to wonder what the surprise might be. Sky nodded at my dark angel, and they both unfurled their glorious wings to their full extent, Sky's glowing white and Phoenix's raven black. Even though Phoenix had told me no one else could see them, I still glanced around nervously.

Sky turned to Caleb and whispered something I couldn't hear, but as I turned to Phoenix, he leaned over and whispered, "With these wings, I promise to love you forever, for better or worse, in sickness and in health, against all odds and with all the power and passion of my heart, body, and soul."

Forgetting where I was, I wrapped my arms around Phoenix's neck and pulled him in for a kiss. Tess grumbled behind us, "Oh for God's sake, get a room, you two." For a moment I lost track of time and my surroundings. I hung from his neck, our lips locked together, his flavor on my tongue, his scent inebriating all my senses. I didn't want to let go. But this was my brother's thunder, not mine.

I pulled away, my feet—that had left the ground—slowly touching the floor and my hands still entangled in Phoenix's hair. His dark eyes had a warmth that made me weak in the knees. "I love you too, Nix. Forever, whatever forever may be for us."

Applause exploded around us, and I realized we were being watched by every eye in the room. Caleb and Sky had turned around, their backs now to the minister, and were clapping along, huge smiles on their faces. Caleb mouthed, "Love you, sis," and the world suddenly settled, the mad spinning of the last few months slowing down to a crawl and allowing me to breathe at ease again.

Phoenix pulled me in for another hug, and then we both walked toward the newlyweds to congratulate them. My angel walked slightly ahead of me, hand stretched in Sky's direction, and something about his outstretched wings caught my eye. I stopped and looked closely, wonder filling my heart.

Here and there, strewn among the dark feathers of his wings, a glint of white was peeking through. I asked him to stop and peered even closer, running my hand over each feather, not quite believing what I was seeing.

"What is it?" Phoenix asked me, alarm in his voice. "Something wrong?"

I choked on a sob. "No, n-nothing wrong," I said, stuttering a bit and lowering my voice so the others wouldn't hear. "On the contrary. Nix, you have white feathers growing in your wings."

Phoenix curled his wings over himself so he could look and let out a gasp when he found the silvery white feathers among the black.

Gabriel stepped up then, his white wings also unfurled in full majesty. "The darkness is receding, angel," he said. The others were all chatting amongst themselves, so I guessed he had put a charm over us. "The phoenix has risen."

# EPILOGUE

## NIX

I am light.

Light is all I know—it's in what I do, what I breathe, what sustains me.

My memories of the time before have faded into the past as joy and love surround me from morning until dawn. The loving whispers, the caresses, the kisses feed my heart and soul. I am alive.

I am reborn. The memories of a time when I didn't love fully and completely are just that—fragments of a time gone by. Forever awaits.

I don't just exist anymore. I thrive—a body and soul full of everything good and wholesome. I wake up and I see light lying beside and inside me.

I'm no longer in darkness. I'm a creature of light and a carrier of hope.

In light I dwell, and light I am.

# ACKNOWLEDGMENTS

Writing a book really takes a village. I don't know where I would be without my editors, my proofreaders, my graphic designers, and everyone else who helped me make this book a reality.

I have to thank my beta readers who helped me refine *Dark Feathers*, especially those who read my book before it was even finished, such as Belinda Miller, Alisha Vincent, and Lisa Meyer. Your insights were invaluable.

My critique group that had to read and critique innumerable excerpts. David, Ann-Marie, Karen, Nicole, and Arlene, thank you so much for all your encouraging words, and also for being honest and pointing out the flaws in the manuscript.

Thanks go to Audrey Hughey from the Author Transformation Alliance, who has supported me with advice and encouragement throughout the whole process, and also to many of the ATA writers for always being there as sounding boards any time I needed one.

A special thank you to the Hot Tree Self-Publishing team for their invaluable help with this project. Olivia, you were awesome as usual. So were all the editors, beta readers, proofreaders, and formatters who I had the privilege to work with. Thank you, Tracey of Soxsational Cover Art for putting up with my pickiness in choosing a cover for my book and still coming up with one I truly love.

To my pub-sisters at Hot Tree, a great big thank you for the amazing support you are always willing to give me. You're not only great writers, you're awesome human beings.

My wonderful and energetic sprint partners, Alisha, Marianne, and Sara, whose virtual company kept me going even when I was too exhausted to think. You guys are true gems. Thank you so much.

Finally, a great big thank you to my sister, Marilia, whose love for everything angelic inspired me in part to write first *Lavender Fields* and then *Dark Feathers*. Love you, sis.

My lovely readers, I'm so grateful for your support. Without you, this would never happen. I hope this book, just like the others before, bring a measure of joy to your daily lives. That's all an author can hope for.

# OTHER WORKS BY
# NATALINA REIS

**MM PARANORMAL ROMANCE**

*Lavender Fields*

*Infinite Blue*

**ROMANTIC COMEDY**

*Loved You Always*

*Blind Magic*

*Her Real Man*

*Fictional-ish*

**ROMANTIC SUSPENSE**

*We Will Always Have the Closet*

**ROMANTIC FANTASY**

***THE JEWEL CHRONICLES***

*Desert Jewel*

*Snow Jewel*

*Rebel Jewel*

**DYSTOPIAN/SCI-FI ROMANCE**

*Heart's Prey*

# ABOUT THE AUTHOR

Natalina wrote her first romance in collaboration with her best friend at the age of thirteen. Since then she has ventured into other genres, but romance is first and foremost in almost everything she writes.

After earning a degree in tourism and foreign languages, she worked as a tourist guide in her native Portugal for a short time before moving to the United States. She's lived on three continents and a few islands, and her knack for languages and linguistics led her to a master's degree in education. She lives in Virginia, where she has taught English as a Second Language to elementary school children for more years than she cares to admit.

Natalina doesn't believe you can have too many books or too much coffee. Art and dance make her happy, and she is pretty sure she could survive on lobster and bananas alone. When she is not writing or stressing over lesson plans, she shares her life with her husband and two adult sons.

### CONNECT WITH NATALINA ONLINE:

Facebook: www.facebook.com/authornatalinareis
Website/Blog: www.natalinareis.com
Twitter: @TichaB
GR: www.goodreads.com/author/show/14883335.Natalina_Reis
Amazon: www.amazon.com/Natalina-Reis/e/B01ADQ9FJW/
BookBub: www.bookbub.com/profile/natalina-reis
Instagram: @reisnatalina
Reader Group: www.facebook.com/groups/215263965917134/
Pinterest: www.pinterest.com/lisboeta62/

9 780578 579788